Red Zone

A Dominion Falls Novel

Sarah Cass

Historical Western Romance

A Divine Roses Ink Book
Historical Western Romance
First E-book Publication: April 2023
First Print Publication: April 2023

Red Zone: A Dominion Falls Novel
Copyright © 2014 Sarah Cass

Cover design by Sarah Cass
Edited by Megan Koenen
Proofread by Mary Terrani

All cover art and logo copyright © 2018 by Sarah Cass

PUBLISHER
Divine Roses Ink
http://www.divinerosesink.com

Other Books in
The Dominion Falls Series

Independent Brake
Changing Tracks
Derailed
Dark Territory
Green Eye
Runaway Train
Home Signal

Coming Soon in
The Dominion Falls Series

Dust Raiser
Chase the Red
Blizzard Lights
Dead Man's Switch
Bird Cage
A Highball Arrangement
Douse the Glim
Blood
Grave Digger
Bad Order

Books by Sarah Cass
The Tribe Series
The Tribe
The Wolf
The Chief
The Raven
The Lake Point Series
Santa, Maybe
Deep-Fried Sweethearts
Stalled Independence
Witch Way
A Thorough Thanksgiving
Eve's New Year
Heartstrings & Hockey Pucks
Luck of the Cowgirl
Stars, Stripes & Motorbikes
Free Falling
Love for Hire
Haunted Hearts
Stand Alone Novels
Masked Hearts
Leap

Dedication

I wrote this novella many moons ago, and it never saw
the light of day until now. I'm happy to bring you, at last,
the story of Leanne and Tom.

This is for all those writers who have thought of giving
up, or have given up.
To the dreamers who think it isn't worth it or it isn't
possible.
I'd given up in recent years.
Thought my books weren't enough, weren't good,
weren't popular.
No, I don't make a lot off them, I'm no insanely popular
author by any means.
But I love my worlds.
I love my characters.

I write for that love. For the love of a world that exists
only in my mind, with characters as real to me as my own
family and friends.
A world that I feel blessed to offer to others.
If only one person reads, then it's worth it to me.

Keep dreaming.
Keep giving those worlds life.
It's worth it…
For your soul.

Chapter 1

Leanne stood in front of the large house, hands on her hips. A whole list of needs and wants filled her head the longer she stood there. The approaching hoof beats gave her the perfect excuse to brush aside her vast, and likely expensive, imaginings.

Her good friend Jane rode toward her slowly, the woman's gaze on the house in front of Leanne. Jane alit from her horse, a smile brightening her features as she approached. "So, is this it?"

"Sure is. What do you think?"

"How many rooms?"

"Not enough. I'll require a meeting with Hammy." Leanne pushed open the gate. "Come on inside, I'll show you what I'm thinking."

"It's a great location, up on the hill like this. Easy access for the wealthier sort."

"That's the plan." Leanne grinned. "No offense to the men about town, but most of them can't afford to even sniff as they walk by, so my prime position near Denny's tavern isn't so prime."

"Ah, but as the largest brothel in town, you have them saving their pennies."

"I don't imagine I'll be the only brothel forever. I need to secure some classier clients before someone else moves in."

"True, although Cole has managed to scare off the first couple of attempts at competition for you, the men are getting restless for something they can afford." Jane followed her into the house, her sharp eyes scanning every detail. "Some days I worry that we made a poor choice to get rid of the brothel."

One year before, Jane and Cole had closed what had once been Cole's saloon and brothel in order to reopen as The Hangman's Inn. They'd either placed the whores elsewhere, or gotten them into other positions within the hotel. They'd helped move Leanne's brothel from Denver to Dominion Falls, but as Leanne ran a high class whorehouse, many of the miners who made so little and saved so much for booze couldn't afford the cost of her whores.

She knew Cole was only running new brothels out of town to help her, and he only did so because of two reasons. One, he had a small interest still in her business. She could have bought it back, but she knew he liked to keep an eye on her because of the other reason. He was her brother, a fact no one in town but Jane and her brother Tommy knew.

Leanne frowned. "I thought business was good at The Hangman's Inn."

"Oh, it's excellent, but the men in town aren't the only ones getting restless." Jane ran her hand along the wall in the hallway. "This needs to go. This space should be wide open to greet your clients. What about a bar area?"

"You read my mind." Leanne moved closer. "But go back for a moment. What do you mean? Cole can't be restless. He has you."

"Oh, not for female company." Jane chuckled. "Not that sort of restless. He misses that business. He was very good at it. He still has an interest in yours, but no one in town does or can know, because they'd wonder why."

"And heaven forbid anyone know I'm his sister. They don't even know Alma is, and she lives with you both."

"Ah, but at least they know she is a relation. You don't even get that privilege."

"As they don't get the privilege to know the two of you are married." Leanne's smile brightened along with Jane's. "Oh, what this town would do if they learned all of Cole's secrets."

"They'd be lost. They'd feel their world had entirely caved in." Jane turned her attention on Leanne, a piercing gaze that made Leanne's stomach quiver. "Speaking of family."

"Oh my goodness, please don't start on me now." Leanne moved up the stairs to partly run away from the line of questioning. "There are only four rooms up here. That is not nearly enough."

"It is for your current staff, if you have a room downstairs for yourself." Jane followed behind close. "And I am not done talking about it."

"I am." Leanne knew Jane meant well, but there was a lot rather intimidating about a possible relationship. Many factors that all meshed into a big ball of 'This is crazy'. She shook her head and addressed the other subject at hand. "I'm bringing in more girls. I have a lead on a pair of twins that are available."

"Twins? Really? That will definitely be a draw, and mean bigger money for the men that want both."

"Exactly. I need to go meet with them in person to be sure they'll be a good fit."

"So how will you add rooms?"

Leanne was relieved that Jane kept the subject changed to something safer than whatever was happening between Leanne and Tommy. She led Jane through the rest of the house. At the back, she pointed out the wide area between the home and barn, the very space she planned to use to add on to the back of the house to add rooms, including a good sized room for herself.

Jane had plenty of advice, having only recently gone through construction on her place. As for decorating, Leanne had plenty of ideas all on her own. She was relaxed by the time they made it to one of the rooms up front. "I think it'll be good for the business. To be surrounded by some true wealth."

"With more coming in ever day thanks to Lillian Daugherty's campaign to make Dominion Falls the place to be." Jane sighed and leaned on the window frame. "Now if only we could attain a proper dressmaker, this town would be near perfect."

"I can't imagine it'll take much longer. Once the theater is completed, someone will be around to ensure everyone is dressed."

"Ah, but will the someone be a decent dressmaker? I've been around Denver enough to see that they are not all so talented."

"We can only hope. While I have a perfectly good dressmaker in Denver that still has my measurements, I do hate sending out for my gowns." Leanne shrugged. "At least she has your measurements as well."

"Too true, although I'm not sure Cole appreciates such a thing. He doesn't care for my predilection toward acquiring so many dresses. On the thin months they are an extravagance."

"Not quite. They are a necessity to your good spirit."

Jane laughed. "I like that. I believe I'll use it next time Cole complains. Although with Sally and Alma in the mix, and soon enough Clara as well, I may have to reduce my spending."

Alma was Leanne's sister who was, to say kindly, not precisely normal. When Alma turned eighteen and could no longer attend the school Cole had ensconced her in for years, Jane had insisted they take her in.

Sally, on the other hand, was another story. She'd been a whore in Cole's brothel, brought in during a time of great stress for Cole and Jane by Cole's former business partner, Graham. When Jane had realized the girl was merely fifteen, she'd refused to continue prostituting her and instead had taken her in as a ward.

Clara was Jane and Cole's daughter, twin to their son Colton. Leanne found her now one year old niece adorable. "Oh, but I certainly help you along with both Alma and Clara. I believe your brothers do their own share of doting. How much are you truly spending on any of them?"

"And Tommy still has a special bond with Sally all these years later."

"She did save his life."

"Exactly." A wicked smirk grew on across Jane's features. "Of course, he has a certain bond with you as well."

"Jane, please."

"Leanne, please. It's been a year. Why aren't you two courting already?"

"It isn't as simple as that. I'm a whore."

"No. No, you aren't." Jane tsked and shook her head. "You are a madam, the owner of a brothel. You, my dear, are a virgin. It is difficult to be a whore if you are a virgin."

"You know as well as I that there is more to it than that. To the town, I am a whore. Tommy is also…there is more to it than that."

Jane sighed dramatically. "As the queen of all things complicated, I must say that you are overstating the situation. Tommy cares for you, and you for him. And yet neither of you will take the next step."

"It's not as simple as you make it to be."

"Are you afraid?"

"No." Though a virgin herself, Leanne had spent a good deal of her life around the business. She'd seen it could be good, and bad, and good some more. She had no illusions of perfection the first time, or every time. Still, after being protected from men herself for so long, it was intimidating to think of suddenly being on the other side. "Not exactly."

"Talk is one thing, action is another." Jane's smile softened into understanding. "I bet he's as 'not afraid' as you are."

"Seems like he is," Leanne all but whispered.

"Speak of the devil." Jane pressed her hands to the window and shoved open. "Thomas! We're up here."

"What do you think of it?" Tommy's grin peeped out from under the brim of his hat as he turned his head toward them.

"I think you did good cluing Leanne into this place. It's going to be profitable for her." Jane half leaned out the window. "Are you coming up?"

Leanne rolled her eyes at Jane's maneuverings. "Leave him be."

"Well, I wouldn't be his sort-of sister if I did." Jane leaned back. "What can I say? I might already have you as my sister-in-law, but it's not publicly known. If you marry Tommy I can proudly call you my sister in law without anyone wondering how or why."

"Marriage? Now you're pushing matters." Leanne's protest cut off as Tommy's heavy boot steps headed up the stairs. She'd kill Jane before this was all over. "Don't you dare say that to him, got it?"

"You're no fun."

"Not even a little bit."

* * * *

Tommy didn't miss much, including the dark look Leanne shot Jane as he entered the room. For her part, Jane's smile proved she was in a fiery mood, a damn dangerous thing anymore. When she'd been Clara, his sister, her fiery moods were easily dispersed. This woman she'd become since amnesia had taken away Clara was a different story.

In many ways he liked the strong spitfire she was now much more than he had Clara. Not to speak ill of the dead, but he was glad that even in amnesia Jane had learned some good lessons from Clara. Even if those didn't include a lick of cooking or housework.

Still, Jne in a mood often meant trouble for him one way or another. He eyed Jane carefully, but spoke to Leanne. "So what did I miss?"

"Nothing," Leanne snapped.

"Not a thing. Leanne was simply giving me a tour and telling me all about the expansion she planned." Jane set her hands on her hips. "You told me nothing of the twins she planned to bring in, Thomas. I thought you were supposed to keep us abreast of all updates. We do have a vested interest in the business, even if it is completely silent."

Tommy furrowed his brow at the question. "Well, that's damn news to me, too, Janey. I didn't know anything about it, you nosy biddy."

"He didn't know. I just learned about them myself." Leanne's bright smile returned, and with it some of Tommy's good mood. That woman got him all tangled up, which was bad. Too many factors turned a fun flirtation into dangerous territory for him, and her. "I was going to head out first thing next week to meet with them."

"I hope you weren't planning on traveling alone." Jane's smile faded into genuine concern.

"I am capable of such things." Leanne laughed. "I have traveled on my own a few times, after all."

"Sorry, of course you have." Jane wiped her palms on her skirts, a nervous habit she'd developed when memories of the maniac that had once tried to kill her emerged.

"And I'm not going too terribly far. The girls are in a little town in Utah. According to their letter, it hasn't grown much in years and the well is rather dry as far as their services." Leanne shrugged. "I should be gone and back in less than two weeks, hopefully with the twins."

"Utah?" Tommy frowned, a sharp eye on Jane when she paled. "Where, exactly?"

"Heber City."

A strangled squeak emerged from Jane, a low muttering filling the air as sweat beaded on her forehead. Tommy moved over to her side, and let her grip his hand tight.

"What is it?" Leanne moved to Jane's other side. "Goodness, you look as though you've seen a ghost."

"It's a coincidence, is all. Right, Tommy?" Jane laughed it off with a tight, nervous chuckle. "You simply caught me off-guard."

"Of course it's a coincidence, Jane." Tommy reassured her without hesitation. The worst of her past had been dealt with and everyone had moved on. "A pretty funny one, too. I bet anything Clara taught the twins she's talking about."

"Pretty certain she didn't teach them that. Although her reputation wasn't any cleaner than mine was, I suppose." Jane dabbed at her forehead. "Oh, I do hate when the past surprises me. You'd think I was used to it by now."

"What are you two talking about?" Leanne's brows puckered in an adorable signal of her confusion. "You knew the twins?"

"No, but Clara probably did." Tommy released Jane so she could finish composing herself. "In a crazy coincidence, Heber City is where Clara met and married David. It's also where she was a teacher for four years before her disappearance."

"Oh, I see." Realization softened the confusion into a smile. "Well, of course there's no conspiracy here. Just a couple of girls looking to make a little more money in a bigger town."

"All the same, I'd feel better if Tommy went. He's familiar with the town, after all he spied on Clara plenty there." Jane shot him a half accusatory look. "And he can reassure me what we all know to be true, that it's simply a coincidence."

Tommy narrowed his eyes at Jane. "So this is all for your sanity."

"Oh, heavens no. I lost that years ago." She smiled too bright, a wicked gleam returning to her eyes. "But safety is more important than ever now that you have a niece and nephew involved, right? Not to mention Sally."

"Sally's nearly an adult now."

"Yes, but she still lives under my roof." Jane stepped forward and laced her arm with Tommy. "Come, we'll make the travel arrangements now."

"The hotel," Tommy protested against her scheming.

"Cole and I can handle things for, what was it you said, Leanne?"

Leanne shuffled along behind them and mumbled, "Under two weeks."

"Brilliant." Jane rubbed his large belly. "We'll have to be sure to have Cora pack plenty of food for the trip. We'd hate to have your girlfriend upset on the train ride."

"Janey," Tommy warned, and brushed aside her hand. "You're pushing your luck."

"I know." At the bottom of the steps, she turned to hug Leanne. "Don't you worry about a thing. We'll get everything set. Meet me for lunch later."

Leanne's protest was lost in her open mouthed surprise. In no time Jane had dragged Tommy to their horses. The woman was stronger than she looked.

Tommy tugged his hand free soon as they got to their horses. "What do you think you're up to?"

"Not a damn thing."

"I thought you didn't lie."

"Fine." Jane rolled her eyes and gave his arm a good tug. "Let's just move. We'll get you both some tickets and reserve a place at a boarding house or something there. I'm sure they don't have a hotel."

"We might have to stay at the brothel. Last I was there I had to. No boarding house to speak of, and if it hasn't grown any." He eyed her suspiciously. "Is this really about it being Heber City?"

"Of course, that's a major part of it. Clara left behind more than David in that little town. I'd rather be safe than sorry over the coincidence. Plus, it gives me a good excuse to be sure Leanne doesn't travel alone."

"That's your own paranoia."

"And she's my dear friend, so she gets to be subjected to it." She climbed the few steps onto the train platform. "And it finally gets you two some time alone without this whole town watching."

"I'm not here to have you play matchmaker."

"I don't have to play anything." She stepped closer to speak in an exceptionally low tone so only he'd hear. "But you two have been dancing for over a year. Whether it's because of Cole watching like a hawk, or her status as a virgin, or what, I don't care. Figure things out one way or the other before you both explode."

"We aren't going to explode," he called after her retreating back. "Meddling little brat is what you are."

"I stick with what I'm good at," she muttered in reply.

"I do wish you'd stick with what you're good at that doesn't involve me."

"We all have wishes and dreams, big brother."

Chapter 2

Tommy kicked back a long swig of whiskey. He dropped the glass on the counter. After it had been refilled, he glared at his friend across the bar. "Your woman is going to be the death of me."

Cole chuckled low and deep, a broad grin stretching across his features. Instead of answering right away, he dried a few glasses. "Give me a minute. I'm just enjoying the fact that it isn't me she's harping on over something or other."

"You're funny. Real funny."

"What's she bothering you about now?"

"What do you think?"

"My guess would be Leanne."

"Yup." Tommy tossed back the latest glassful of whiskey. "Like she doesn't have anything better to do with her time than harp on me. What with all of those kids, not to mention you, this hotel and that library."

"Figured you'd slip right through them cracks, did you?" Cole shook his head and propped his hands on the bar. "My woman don't miss a trick."

"I know all too well." Tommy wiped down his mouth and let out a long sigh. "She's got me going to Heber City with Leanne to pick up some new girls."

"Heber City? Is that right? Isn't that where Davie and Clara got all cozy?"

Tommy had to admit, he was impressed at how Jane had managed to change Cole's vernacular over time. Though it still carried quite a bit of the rough miner talk, he'd really learned to tone it down. Tommy nodded. "Where they met, carried on a brief scandalous affair that led to their brief, tragic marriage."

"That's why she's got you following along?"

"That and…other reasons."

"You know what?" Cole leaned forward. "Don't let her know I said this, but Jane's right."

"Trust me, I won't say a word. The last thing she needs to be thinking is she's right. She's already a giant pain in my ass half the time." Tommy rubbed his hand over his face. "And you agreeing with her isn't helping me one bit. You're supposed to be my friend, you know."

"I just never picked you as a yellow belly."

Tommy tensed at the implication and stood to meet his friends eyes. "Pardon?"

"You heard me. Never pegged you as yellow. Afraid to get with Leanne."

"I'm not afraid, and I resent the implication. There are extenuating circumstances."

"What?"

Tommy half chuckled-half groaned as he returned to his seat. "It's complicated with things you know I can't talk about publicly."

"Complicated?" Cole snorted. "Don't talk to me 'bout complicated. I got to deal with your sister and all her ugly business, not to mention her brothers."

"Yeah, yeah." Tommy chuckled. "At least one of us is all right."

"Yeah, the one that lives far away." Cole grinned. "I don't gotta put up with him making sure I'm not doing something wrong all the time."

"Oh, you do plenty wrong." Jane interrupted Tommy's planned reply. She bore a wicked smirk, and surprisingly had no children with her. "However, I rather enjoy many of the wrong things we do together."

"Thought you said they weren't wrong." Cole tugged her against him soon as she got behind the bar.

"Not to me, they aren't." She laughed and kissed him deeply. "Now come on, remind me what some of them are. I'm certain Thomas won't mind tending bar for you."

"Says you. I might have plans." He didn't, but Tommy had no designs on making things easy on them. "Besides, I thought you were thoroughly busy today. That's what you said when you barked at me to get up and at'em this morning."

"I did, but miracles do happen. Michael and Daisy are minding the twins, Sally is on a picnic with Arthur." A slow smile curved across Jane's lips as she cast a sideways glance at Cole. "And even Alma is occupied, as Jesse, Isaac and Cindy took her fishing. Tommy leaves tomorrow and we won't have another chance for two whole weeks for midday pleasures."

"Take over," Cole said without another glance at Tommy. The couple were lost in each other before they'd made it to the door that led to their apartment.

Happy as he was to see Jane so content, Tommy didn't enjoy watching them paw at each other. After all, Jane was still his sister even if she was no longer technically Clara. A short shriek drew his attention back in time to see Cole shut the door, Jane flung over his shoulder.

Tommy chuckled and shook his head. He could have been stubborn and moody about having the bar and gambling floor foisted on him, but he didn't have much else to do that day. Jane had a point that he was leaving and they'd be forced to manage the place themselves constantly without him to back them up.

Part of him was happy for the chance to be traveling again, to stretch his legs a bit. The past two years had been the first time he'd been consistently still since the war. Whenever he had an opportunity to move about and do something different was good.

Then there was the issue of Leanne. While he was certainly interested in her, painfully so at times, there were a couple of big factors involved. For example, the fact that despite his public show of indifference toward her, Cole was exceptionally protective of his secret half-sister.

Cole's influence was why the other factor existed—Leanne's virginity. Well-versed though she may be able to act in the art of her trade as madam to a full whorehouse of skilled women, words and talk didn't compare to the actual act.

Tommy wasn't sure he could, or cared to, be the one to introduce reality into that sort of buildup. Years of whispers, learning, and imaginings could deal a hard blow to what it was really like most of the time.

Of course, there was also another mitigating factor. Much as he cared for Leanne, he didn't dare care for her more. His first marriage had been disastrous—and he bore the blame for its destruction. He'd been a Pinkerton and about everything took precedence over their marriage.

He wasn't so sure he'd changed all that much.

"Morning Tommy. Seen Janey this morning?" A familiar voice interrupted his musings. The wrinkled, ruddy features of Gilbert Hamm grinned at him from across the bar. The old man had a crush on Jane, and she had a soft spot for him.

Tommy grinned, glad for the distraction. "Just saw her head to the back with Cole. You after something, or just want a glimpse?"

Hammy offered a gap-toothed grin. "She wanted me to go over some plans update the barn or something. Said Cole needs better space to work."

"She just wants to be able to see the corral from their apartment so she can see Cole working the horses. She didn't think that all through when planning this place out." Tommy chuckled. "She was too focused on the hotel and not Cole's little side career and what it does for her libido."

When Tommy set a beer in front of him, Hammy didn't hesitate to scoop it up even though he hadn't voiced the request aloud. "We was supposed to meet at the library, but she weren't there. Kat told me she'd be here."

"She'll be along soon enough. Enjoy your beer while you wait." Tommy tapped the bar, his attention drawn to the door when another figure passed through. He nodded at Leanne with a smile. "Are you looking for Jane as well?"

"Are you kidding? I was there when Michael suggested he and Daisy take the twins. The woman fairly flung her children at the fool in her rush to get back here." Leanne laughed and patted the bar. "Whiskey, please. I came to relax for a bit. The negotiations over the property were intense this morning."

Tommy frowned, he'd thought Leanne had only to sign papers on the new property. "How so? I thought it was more a meeting to sign papers than to negotiate."

"So did I. Apparently your brother thought different." Leanne smirked. She'd used one of Tommy's other brothers, Nick, to make the deal. As he was a lawyer, it had made sense, but Tommy's tension rose because there'd been a flirtation between the two off and on.

"That so?"

"He said something about flood risk, and water lines, and it was all very dramatic. Rather amusing to see him get a spark of something."

"That so?" Tommy forced out a grin.

"He managed to knock another three hundred dollars off the purchase price. So I'm not complaining over his theatrics." Leanne chuckled. "I thought I'd invite you to lunch, but then I stumbled on Jane getting relieved of the twins and figured that was out of the question."

Tommy relaxed when she mentioned lunch. "True. I've got to watch the place. I'll be free for supper, though."

"Supper it will be, then. Shall I tell Cora to send you some food?" Leanne downed her whiskey without losing a beat. "I'd hate for you to fill up on whiskey alone."

"I was going to have someone do that, if you could on your way out, it'd be appreciated."

"Consider it done." Leanne winked and rose. She gave Hammy a peck on the cheek, sending the man into a fit of blushing. "Hammy."

"Miss Leanne." Hammy fidgeted in his seat.

When she'd left, Tommy gave him a pointed glance. "You're going to make Jane jealous you keep that up."

"Aw, Tommy. It ain't like that."

"Of course it isn't, Hammy. Of course it isn't."

* * * *

Poor Hammy.

Leanne folded her skirt with great care to be sure everything fit into the two bags she was taking instead of a trunk. Jane, the clothes hound, had lamented Leanne's decision.

"What about this one?" Jane sat awash in a virtual sea of colorful cotton and lace. At the moment she held up a yellow and blue striped underskirt that Leanne knew to be one of Jane's favorites.

"Jane, I will hardly be gone long enough for all the outfits you are suggesting." Leanne sighed as she scanned the bed covered in her dresses, Jane in the middle. Unfortunately the building she'd bought on first arriving did not have the room for the same sort of closet she'd had in Denver. While her new place would, in the mean time she was overloaded.

"I know, but this is one that is rather exceptional." Jane leaned over and burrowed under some petticoats. The woman had admired Leanne's vast closet so much that Cole had built her one as a surprise. "I know I saw a lovely yellow overskirt and bodice to accompany it."

"Keep it." Due to her status as the owner of a high class brothel, most of Leanne's day to day outfits fit well in proper society, including the one Jane searched for. While in their lounge alone Leanne and her girls wore far more revealing outfits, one of which Jane owned, outside the building they were to never appear crass or too revealing. It was their job to suit the higher classes, and they wore their exteriors well.

"What?" Jane straightened, her eyes wide with surprise even as a grin played at her lips. Despite her eager grin, she shook her head. "I couldn't."

"Of course you could." Leanne tsked, her scolding interrupted by her own laughter. "You have been admiring that dress from the moment I added it to my wardrobe. I hardly wear it because I fear you salivating over it."

"Salivating over what?" Kat entered without so much as a knock, her unruly red curls in exceptional fashion. On any given day, Kat kept her curls under some sort of control, but it appeared for the moment she'd given up the fight.

While Leanne tried to form a response with some sort of decorum, Jane had no such luck. Jane's bold laughter rang through the room and when Leanne turned back, Jane was rolling with laughter. Tears shimmered as she pointed at Kat.

Kat patted the mess, faint pink seeping into her cheeks. "Cindy and Lizzie asked to take care of my hair for me. I didn't have the heart to fix it once they left for school. It's painfully out of control, I'm afraid."

Leanne's laughter joined Jane's and she nodded. "I'm afraid so. Let's see if we can do something so Jane can stop laughing and breathe again, shall we?"

"I haven't been able to figure anything out that won't mess up their, um, style choice."

With a wide ribbon she often used as a decorative belt in hand, Leanne moved behind Kat. After some struggle she managed to tie the ribbon over the crown of Kat's head and then loop the back into a broad ponytail of frizzy curls. "It's still rather poufy, but it's better."

Jane's laughter eased, though hiccupping giggles escaped in between breaths. "It is somewhat better. Oh my."

"The things we do for our children." Kat cleared her throat. "Now, what is it Jane was salivating over before my hair made its entrance?"

Jane chuckled, but didn't lose control again as she lifted the skirt in question. "This."

"Oh, yes. I swear she was planning a great heist to swipe that dress from your closet." Kat smirked. "It was an elaborate plan that involved some rather unusual assistance if I remember correctly."

"Oh, pshaw. I did no such thing." This time it was Jane's turn to blush. "And even if I did, it was all in good fun."

"Either way, it's yours. No great heist needed. Perhaps I'll get something new when we pass through Denver or Ogden." Leanne placed the skirt she'd carefully folded into the bag. "That's as good a reason as any to leave some space in my bag and closet. Plus, you really adore that dress, and it should take little to no altering to fit. We are of a similar size."

"I shouldn't." Even as she spoke, Jane clutched the skirt closer.

"Please do." Leanne chuckled. "At least this time Cole can't complain about the expense of a new dress, as you didn't have to pay for that one."

"And it has been a while since I've had a chance to wear something new," Jane agreed.

Kat shook her head. "You and your clothes. I'm telling you, pants are the way to go. Your fashion choices are far easier, and you get attention wherever you go." She turned this way and that, flashing her scandalously trousered legs.

"I cause enough scandal without wearing trousers, and I enjoy the fashion, thank you." Jane rose off the bed, the skirt and matching bodice and overskirt in hand. "I'd enjoy it more with a proper seamstress in town."

"You and mother both. She won't move here until we have one, so I'm holding out hope it takes some time." Kat leaned on the dresser as Jane disappeared behind the screen to change. She turned her attention to Leanne. "And are you prepared for some alone time with Tommy?"

Leanne groaned and sank to the bed. "Not you too. With all the talk things have become rather awkward of late. It is a business trip for me to pick up a couple of new girls for the brothel, not an elopement or anything of the sort."

"Well, that's what I mean. You will have some time without all of us watching to see when you'll finally get up the gumption to do something. Either of you." Kat smirked. "The whole town's been watching since that day…"

Leanne's lips twitched when Kat's smile faltered. They both knew what she meant, the day he'd been shot going after his old friend who had raped a pregnant Jane. The townspeople assumed he'd gotten drunk, because no one could know what had happened that fateful day. Never before had she been so scared when she'd seen him so injured.

She shook off the mention and shook her head. "Things are not always so easy as they seem. You of all people should know that, Kat."

"I suppose." Kat gasped, the smile returning to her features. "Oh, Jane. It suits you."

Jane turned, the dress sitting well on her frame, though the sleeves were a smidge short. "I'll have to see if Sally can add some lace or blue binding to the wrists to add some length. She's a whiz with a needle."

"Speaking of which. She's growing up fast. Any sign she'll be moving on?" Leanne was happy for the change of subject away from her own romantic life.

"She's not finished with schooling, and she's barely sixetten. Her courtship with Arthur is progressing. However, I think she'll be around another year or two. Besides, Arthur has designs on going to college to be a journalist. She'll have her own decision to make in a year or two." Jane turned in front of the mirror. "It is lovely, Leanne. Thank you."

"Don't mention it." Leanne waved it off. "It suits you well."

"As a token of gratitude I won't tease you about Tommy anymore before you leave."

"I'll accept that token." Leanne sagged in relief. Truth be told, Kat's point had been well made. The watchful eyes of her dear friends, and family, did make things uncomfortably close. Perhaps the trip would do them well.

A girl could hope.

Chapter 3

Leanne jolted awake when the stagecoach hit a brutal bump in the road. A low chuckle beside her drew her attention to her traveling companion. She frowned at him. "Is there something amusing?"

"You snore." Tommy grinned, arms folded across his chest. As the coach rocked again, he managed to stay upright while the rest of the passengers swayed under the movement.

"I do not," she demurred.

"Sure do. Real cute too. Almost a whisper, or like a kitten would."

"You're comparing me to a kitten?" She didn't know whether to laugh or be offended by the likeness. "Are you daft?"

"Depends on who you ask. Jane'll tell you I'm mad as the day is long. Some of my old bosses would say I'm crafty, but definitely not daft."

She hummed her disapproval of his teasing and lifted the curtain on the window to lend some more fresh air to the stuffy cabin. "How long now?"

"You woke just in time, actually. We should be in town in about five minutes." Tommy checked his pocket watch. "Assuming the driver's estimate was correct at last check."

"Thank heavens." Leanne groaned and stretched her sore muscles. She'd not ridden in a stagecoach in years. Most often she preferred to go where the trains did to avoid such a turmoil. Every jolt from the past two days rattled her bones until she felt old as a crone. "I need to stretch my muscles for a day or twenty after this."

"That so? Sore?"

"I feel like I was rode hard and put up wet." She sighed, a wicked thought coming to her head. Before she could stop herself and cast Tommy a sideways look. "And not the way I prefer to be, either."

"What?"

"I mean, it would be different if I'd spent the night enjoying my pleasures, but this is just cruel." She twitched her lips to cover her laughter as all the men in the carriage coughed and shifted in their seats. The one other woman chose to ignore Leanne completely as she had from the start. It always surprised Leanne at how fast other women could peg a whore from a mile away.

Unbelievably, Tommy himself had gone mute. Slack-jawed and wide-eyed, he didn't take his eyes off her for a moment. As the stagecoach slowed and buildings appeared outside the window, he shook his head and cleared his throat. "Ahem. Yes. Well."

Leanne sighed at the uncomfortable tension that rose between them once the line crossed to sexual teasing. At the start they'd had no trouble teasing and joking, but once things drew toward seriousness a wall had built between them.

She missed the way things used to be. This uncomfortable sensation was becoming unbearable. The more their friends and family pushed matters, the worse it got. She guessed there was something else, perhaps the same thing that gave her pause, but she could bear it no longer.

The stagecoach drew to a stop, and amidst more uncomfortable mutterings the rest of the passengers set about to disembark. She didn't move, and was relieved to see that Tommy didn't either at first.

As she wondered what to do to finally break through that uncomfortable tension that kept arising, she realized the answer was in front of her all the time. All she had to do was consider what Jane would have done in the situation.

Nervous flutters flickered across her stomach, but she came up with a bold plan. She turned toward Tommy, and as he opened his mouth to speak, she didn't give him a chance. Quick as a flash she grasped him around the neck and pulled him into a bold kiss.

Before he had a moment to react, either by returning the kiss or pushing her away, she pulled free of the buss. She grinned as he lingered frozen where he sat. "There. Now that that's out of the way, I can go about my business."

She hopped down from the coach with barely a touch to the driver's hand. Somehow the bold move emboldened her and left her almost giddy. What fun she could have if she continued on this path.

How had she allowed things to get so uncomfortable in the first place? She'd never had trouble with men. Then again, she'd never dealt with a man she wasn't out to deceive.

Determined to not let her ponderings ruin her good mood, she pushed the thoughts away to favor the smile she still bore. She strolled along the street, taking in the small town in curiosity. Though she'd been told there was little to it, she was surprised at how true it was.

The wide streets were quiet, no people out and about as they would be back home. No shouting or calling, no ruckus of any sort. The sensation was almost eerie after so many years in Denver and then Dominion Falls. Both the city she'd lived in and the town she now called home always seemed to have something going on, no matter the time of day.

"How odd."

"What's that?" Tommy appeared to have recovered his senses and approached, though his hat was drawn low to hide his eyes.

"It's so quiet here. Does anyone even live here?"

"Not many folks here comparatively. Some farms and ranches outside of the town." He gestured. "Saloon's this way. Driver said it hasn't moved. I imagine that's where you'll find your new girls."

"Yes, I'm sure it is. You've seen to our bags?"

"They'll be sent over."

"Good. All right, then." To be honest, all Leanne wanted at the moment was a good hot bath and an even better night's sleep. She imagined the latter would be more difficult, as the beds in the saloon were likely nothing to write home about.

Inside the saloon only a few patrons sat around. Whores draped about lazily, one even slept soundly in the corner, snoring far less delicately than Tommy had suggested Leanne did. The barkeep stared them down suspiciously.

She approached the bar without hesitation. "Hello. I'm looking for Loren."

"What's it to ya?" He stared down his nose at her.

"My name is Leanne DuBois. We've been corresponding by wire, I believe." Leanne narrowed her eyes briefly.

"Don't think so." He went back to wiping down glasses.

Leanne straightened, her frown deepening. If she hadn't been corresponding with him, things were about to get tricky.

As she opened her mouth to speak, Tommy interrupted. "We need rooms to stay in, and the lady would like a bath."

"Thomas," She muttered. Touched as she was that he stated she wanted, she didn't like being spoken for. This was her business she was dealing with and if she lost any bit of power now, she'd never get it back. "I can take care of myself, thank you."

"We don't got rooms."

"You did last I stayed here. Been about ten years now, I suspect." Tommy leaned on the bar. "It's been a long journey and we need a place to stay. We'll pay well."

Leanne kicked Tommy and threw him a glare.

He gave a subtle shake of his head, keeping his focus on Loren. "We'll make do with one room if you've got it."

Loren shrugged and dug out a key from under the counter. "Top of the stairs, second on the right. Don't got no bath. There's a swimming hole down at the creek, though."

"That'll do," Leanne interjected before Tommy could speak for her again. She snatched the key from the counter. After a glare at Tommy she spun on her heel and headed up the stairs to the room Loren mentioned.

Tommy's footsteps followed her up, but she ignored him in favor of making it to the room.

At the door, she unlocked it and spun to face Tommy. With a smirk, she slammed the door in his face.

"Leanne."

"I told you not to speak for me. Find your own damn room."

* * * *

Out of respect for her anger and pride, Tommy did his best to find another room to stay in. Short of bribing the man in charge of the saloon, he had no luck. If only Leanne would give him a few minutes to explain himself—it probably wouldn't do him any good.

He'd thought he was diffusing the situation by asking for a room. Clearly something was up since the saloon owner, Loren, wasn't exactly happy to see her. Hell, the man wasn't even admitting he'd sent the telegrams. Tommy was hoping to address this curious development before Leanne forced the issue.

Unfortunately, instead of succeeding, he'd gotten himself in deep shit with her. He blamed the kiss for throwing him off balance. Where had that come from?

After almost a year of the tension forming between them, she'd just up and kissed him. Then before he could enjoy it she'd left him high and dry.

The woman had thrown him all off balance. He wasn't used to be thrown off balance. His first wife hadn't been enough distraction to pull him from his job much as she wished. Leanne, on the other hand, was enough to distract him from just about anything, even more so when she was feeling her oats.

To let her cool down, and to get his head back on straight, Tommy had left in search of some place to stay until he got back on her good side. Not surprisingly, he'd had no luck.

He was left with little choice than to beg forgiveness and a patch of floor in Leanne's room. All he had to do was turn on the charm, and be honest about his apology. She'd forgive him.

At the top of the stairs, two whores past him the way down. They giggled and whispered as they made their way to the main floor. He narrowed his eyes at their departing backs, wondering what that was all about.

He stopped at Leanne's door and knocked gently, just enough to get her attention if she was awake. She'd been exhausted when they'd arrived, there was a good chance she was asleep.

"Psst." Two doors away, a whore waved to him. She closed the door to the room she'd just left. Rather than speak aloud, she continued to whisper. "She ain't there."

"Damn." He dropped his hand and glared at the door. "You don't happen to know where she went do you?"

"I do. She went to the swimming hole to bathe." The whore drew closer and leaned against the wall. "I also know it ain't Loren that sent her that telegram. The girls want out, and he don't wanna let them go."

Tommy frowned, he'd suspected as much. "How'd they get the telegram out?"

"Are ya kiddin'? Ya gotta ask how a pair of twin whores got a young, nervous, lonely little man to send some wires?"

"I guess I don't."

"Well, Johnny found out they were givin' favors—"

"Johnny?"

"Man about town that favors them. Runs the bank. He ain't good to them, though. They gotta get patched up after he's done with them."

His stomach turned. Whorehouses were a part of life in most towns, only thing that bothered him about them was when the whores were treated bad. He was impressed at how Cole had always handled things when he'd run the brothel. Clearly Loren wasn't any good. "Damn. So he found out they were giving favors?"

"Made sure Loren found out." She stepped closer, her voice dropped to a whisper. "He's gonna try to get ya to leave. Johnny promised big money for keeping them around."

"So getting to them, and getting them out is gonna be tricky."

Footsteps on the stairs made her jump. A slow smile curved her lips and she leaned into him with a sigh. "Got any plans to indulge? I'm sure Loren'll let ya use a room if ya use one of us."

"Good of you to offer, but I got things handled."

"Handling yourself gets old sometimes."

Tommy chuckled, he sure couldn't argue with that. "Maybe so, but I'll stick with things the way they are."

"Suit yourself." She shrugged and wandered off downstairs.

He pondered his best course of action. If he waited until she returned, he was likely to get the door shut in his face. Might be best to cut her off at the pass and get things clear.

Unless much had changed in the past decade, the swimming hole would be north of town, on the route toward Clara and David's old homestead. Instead of turning west toward that place, though, he'd turn east and go about a quarter mile.

He walked the distance quick as he could, glad he didn't cross her on the way. It would be best to discuss the matter in private, without prying eyes.

Tommy wasn't over-quiet about his approach to the swimming hole. Last thing he wanted to do was surprise her and make his situation worse. As he neared the creek, he opened his mouth to speak, but never got the chance.

A Derringer leveled at his face, a dripping wet, barely covered Leanne glared at him. "Tommy! What in the hell do you think you're doing?"

Chapter 4

Tommy kept his hands half-raised in the air. He didn't think Leanne would really shoot him, but until she got her nerves back under control, he wasn't about to push his luck. "I got some new information. I was coming to tell you."

"Traipsing through the woods like a wild boar? You scared me half to death." Leanne dropped the weapon, but not her glare. "You're lucky I didn't fire my weapon first."

"I was being loud so you'd know I was coming. I figured you'd be madder if I snuck up on you while you were bathing."

"You were wrong both ways. Didn't you think to call out so I knew who it was?" She huffed and turned away to tuck her weapon away. Either she hadn't realized, or didn't care, that the chemise she'd thrown on did nothing to hide one bit of her. Because she was soaking wet when she'd put it on, the muslin clung to her skin and was all but invisible.

Tommy tensed his jaw against the rising groan as his body automatically responded to the sight of her enticing curves. He clasped his hands together to keep from reaching toward her, trying to focus on her anger instead of her breasts as she turned back toward him.

"You don't have anything to say for yourself?"

He blinked a few times and lifted his gaze to the sparkling fury of hers and grinned. "It would have been worth dying if this was the last sight I would have seen." The words escaped before he could think clearly, and he immediately regretted them.

Her jaw dropped, then her gaze to her own body. A little squeak erupted before she lifted her gaze again. A long minute passed where he couldn't tell if she was pissed or amused, and figured it was probably a bit of both when she finally burst out laughing. "I didn't have time to prepare to greet you properly, you overly thoughtless buffoon."

"I'd apologize, but not sure I can." Glad to have her laughing, he joined in. "Maybe I should surprise you more often."

"I wouldn't suggest it. I was a heartbeat away from firing."

"Still would have been worth it. I've survived worse than a shot from a Derringer."

"Don't remind me." Her laughter faded as she turned back to her clothes and gathered them up. "I was there for one of them."

Tommy remembered all too well the one she meant. Not long after they'd met he'd been forced to hunt down a man he'd once thought a friend and dispense justice. Unfortunately, the former friend had also once been a Pinkerton like Tommy had been, and had managed to get a bullet in Tommy's shoulder before he and Cole had ended him.

That day he'd imbibed on a fair lot of moonshine to dull the pain until he could be cared for by a doctor. Leanne and Jane had been waiting on their return, and Leanne had remained at his side while his brother Charlie took care of getting the bullet out.

"Hey, I've been good since. I've gone well over a year without getting shot."

"You say that like it should be considered an accomplishment of some sort." Leanne resituated her skirts, tossing him a smirk before she grabbed her vest. "You know I've managed to go my whole life without getting shot once. There might be something wrong with your family as it seems they've all been shot."

"You don't have room to talk. Cole has a few scars of his own."

"Well, Cole can be an idiot. He's better at protecting others than his own numb skull."

"Good point." Tommy fell into step beside her when she started toward town, her boots in hand. "I got some information from one of Loren's whores."

"Do I care to know how you got the information?" Her cheeks darkened at the question, and she avoided his gaze.

"I was looking for you, she offered it up. I think she's worried about the twins."

"Why would she be?"

"I guess they sent those telegrams, not Loren." Tommy stopped when she did, glad they were still a good distance from any buildings where they might be overheard. "Used their wiles to get him to send them and get the responses to them."

"And Loren found out?"

"I'm guessing so. The girl said they're going to get Loren some real money from the banker, but he likes to hurt them."

"Damn." She set her hands on her hips. Her jaw worked as she stared toward town, deep in thought. "He likes to hurt them?"

"That's what the word is."

"That might just be my bargaining chip." She smiled and dropped her hands from her hips. "Thank you for the information."

"Am I forgiven?"

"Are you going to stop treating me like you own me?"

"I didn't mean to. I swear." He stepped closer and nudged her. "I just wanted to get us information since he was acting so sketchy."

"Next time ask to speak with me. You step all over me and I lose any bit of power I have."

"You're right. I was wrong. You just left me flustered with that kiss."

Another swath of delicate pink filled her cheeks. "You are trying to soften me so you can sleep on my floor."

"I'd rather sleep in your bed."

"Oh. Well." Whatever her flustered answer might have been, it was cut off by a wild scream from the direction of town. The color drained from her features. Without another word, she turned and ran toward town.

Tommy didn't wait to object, not that he would have. The screams continued, and as he got closer he realized it was two voices, young ones if he was to guess right. The made it into the heart of town and found the street cluttered for the first time since they'd arrived.

Everyone's attention was directed at the south end of the street. Off in the distance the schoolhouse stood, a small cluster of children gathered outside staring back toward town.

In between the schoolhouse and the crowd a handful of army soldiers surrounded two children. It was the children making the ruckus, fighting tooth and nail to try to get away from the group. Once the group stopped, the screaming ceased as well.

The larger of the children, a girl, gathered the boy close to her. Her wide green eyes scanned the gathering crowd, her lips curled into a snarl. Though their skin was sun-darkened, the two were clearly white children.

If Tommy had to guess, he'd say the girl was maybe twelve to fourteen, the boy maybe seven, ten at the oldest. They were dressed like Indians, similar to the Ute garb he'd seen years before. Both of the children were clearly terrified.

Leanne's hand grabbed his wrist, her nails dug in hard enough to smart. "Those poor souls," she whispered.

The sergeant in the front of the group scanned the crowd. "These children were found among a roaming band of Injuns in the area. We've been tasked with bringing them here."

"We don't want 'em," someone in the crowd called out. The rest of the group started to rumble in agreement. "Look at them, they're all but savage."

"They're white children, they'll remember the right way to act." The sergeant stepped aside. "They need a place to stay. We can't keep them on the reservation, they're not Injun."

Silence settled over the crowd. Clearly no one wanted them.

Tommy would offer if he was staying in the area, or was in any position to do so.

"Do something," Leanne whispered.

"Like what?"

"I don't know. Anything."

* * * *

Leanne could hardly believe the way everyone around the scene looked as though they'd rather eat cow patties than get anywhere near the children. As a stranger in town, not to mention her status as a whore, she wasn't capable of much.

Still, she felt compelled to do something. She gasped, "What about Jane?"

"You're kidding, right?" Tommy glanced her way. He spoke low and quiet so as to not draw attention. "Given where they come from, you think she'd be any more willing than this lot?"

"Yes." Leanne knew how Jane felt about Indians, but these were children. "Soon as she saw them, she'd have no doubt."

"Wish I could say I thought you were right." Tommy cleared his throat and spoke over the silence. "What of their kin?"

"We don't know that they got any. Won't speak nothing but Injun." The sergeant focused on him. "Might be from 'round here. Might not. Don't know if the lot's been traveling or not."

Leanne frowned. "Well, they're terrified. If they even do remember English, they need to be reassured they're safe."

"They ain't," someone muttered nearby.

"Who'll take 'em?" The sergeant glanced around. "Where's your reverend?"

"Right here." An elderly man that hardly seemed strong enough to haul the two anywhere stepped out. "We'll see to their well-being until we can find someone to take them in."

Leanne released Tommy's hand and moved forward as half the crowd dispersed. She knelt in front of the two children and smiled. "Hello. I'm Leanne."

The girl's lip-curling snarl eased a slight amount. She spat out a slew of words in a language Leanne didn't understand.

"Sounds like Ute," came the kind voice of the reverend. "Won't do either of them much good here, though."

"They need to calm down, maybe get a bath. Tommy, do you have any candy?" Leanne glanced back, but he was in a discussion with the sergeant. "Well, we'll have to see about getting you some candy, won't we? Maybe some good solid food, too."

"Won't be much I can do. The wife died a few years back." The Reverend sighed.

"We'll help how we can," Tommy interjected before Leanne could speak. "Isn't there anyone in town that would take them in?"

"With the reservation so close, likely not. There was a mass escape attempt a few years back, killed a lot of townspeople. You won't find much sympathy here, even for white children raised by them." The reverend held out his hand. "I'm Reverend McGonagall."

"Tommy Young. This here's Leanne." Tommy left off her last name, and Leanne didn't argue. This time she understood and was happy to let the reverend assume she might be his wife.

"Young. Young, sounds familiar. Oh yes, we once had a teacher here by the name. Wonderful young woman. Disappeared a long time ago, we never knew what happened." Reverend McGonagall shook his head as his voice trailed off. After a few blinks he seemed to clear the thoughts and looked hopefully at them both. "Would the two of you?"

"I wish we could. We're strangers here, and without knowing who the children might be, it would be wrong to move them about." Leanne frowned again, her thoughts once again going to Jane. "If we could just help them get settled, perhaps someone would take them."

"If we don't find someone, I will have to send them to Denver."

Tommy sighed. "Let me look around. See if I can't figure out whose kids they are. No matter what, we won't let them get sent to Denver."

The whole time they spoke, the girl's gaze flickered between them. Her attentiveness to their words made Leanne wonder if she might remember English.

As Leanne got ready to approach the girl, a stranger interrupted. "Reverend. Lucy and I'll take 'em. Lucy won't mind none."

A frown flickered across the reverend's features, but he straightened. "Jacob. I haven't seen Lucy in some time. You said she's ill. Are you sure she's up to such a thing?"

"Sure. She's doing better. Talking about coming back to church." Something about this Jacob made Leanne uncomfortable, but she couldn't put her finger on what it was. "We don't mind. They'd have food, a place to sleep, and work to do while ya look for their ma and pa."

"That's more than they'd have at the church." McGonagall seemed reluctant himself, but didn't have any apparent direct objection. "I'll be out to visit them all the time."

"For as long as I'm here, so will I." Leanne spoke before she thought too hard on it.

Tommy clasped her arm, but didn't voice an objection out loud. "Reverend, I'd like to help in the search for their kin."

"Would be much appreciated, Mr. Young. I have some ideas, some families lost in the mass escape a few years back."

McGonagall took a deep breath. "Will you be all right to take them home alone, Jacob?"

"No problem." He approached the kids and took their arms. Low and quiet he spoke in the girls ear, so low Leanne couldn't hear what he said.

Though it all made Leanne uneasy, the children said nothing. The girls wide green eyes lingered on Leanne until she was led out of sight. Leanne swallowed against the lump in her throat. "I'd like to check on them tomorrow, Tommy."

"We will. You all right? I'd like to chat with the reverend here for a bit." Tommy gave her elbow another squeeze. "Leanne?"

"Yes, of course. I'll meet you back at the room." Leanne waved him off, her gaze fixed where the three had disappeared. She sighed, knowing there was little else she could do. Just because she felt uneasy didn't mean there was anything wrong. She was simply concerned because the children had been traumatized enough.

She'd give it a few days and see how they did, and if they had no leads, she'd contact Jane. Surely Jane would sympathize with their plight.

Leanne shook off the unease she felt in the pit of her stomach best as she could. Tomorrow she'd check on the children again. For the moment she other matters to deal with.

Like what to do about the twins.

Chapter 5

Leanne's original plan was to confront the owner straight away, but then she thought better of it. Much as she would appreciate a quick end to the matter, it might be best to get some information first.

Soon as she entered the brothel, Loren fixed her with a dark stare again. Whether for her attempt to retain the twins, or from her actions with the children outside, she couldn't be sure. A few men in the room took notice of her as well, so she kept her Derringer clutched in one hand as she passed through without acknowledging one of them.

Though her mind was caught up in thoughts of the twins, and the children the army had brought in, she kept some attention on the men in the saloon. At least one rose when she got to the stairs and she held her breath. Tommy wasn't with her for any measure of protection.

One of the lounging whores swept across the room and distracted the man. Grateful she didn't have need to draw her weapon, she darted up the steps to her room.

Leanne paced the room, pondering her best plan of action. For the time being she was little more than an encroachment on his turf, one that could potentially take away a surge of income from him. While she had a few arguments for her case, the last thing she needed to do was approach him while he had backup and she had none.

Then again, if she waited, would she appear weak? Who was she kidding? As a woman, that was automatically assumed.

That left her with her original plan, though not the best option. She would have to straighten herself up and go down to face Loren. She checked herself in the grimy mirror, knowing her still-damp hair was likely rather unruly.

She set about fixing the wet mess into a presentable knot. With practice skill she drew her brush through the length, twisting and braiding as she moved. Until she was left with several long braids that needed to be set into place. Along with her two favored, heavy thick switches that would help her hair cover her head in its most elaborate, thick knots.

If she was going to do this, she would go all out. Soon as her hair was piled on her head and pinned in place, she grabbed her powders. Using the small mirror within her compact, she applied her makeup as if she were managing a room full of men in her occupied brothel.

When she'd left she thought Jane mad for making her pack one of her nicest dresses, but now she was relieved. Leave it to Jane to think of everything.

She donned her finest, and at last felt ready to be what she knew she was capable of—a strong woman of business. After all, she'd spent years in the business of men. She knew how to study them and work their weaknesses.

When she'd arrived in town she'd been exhausted, sore, and filthy. Granted, she still hadn't had any sleep, the dip in the swimming hole had done wonders for the other issues at hand. At the very least, she felt more capable of handling herself now.

She flung open the door, ready to confront the brothel owner, only to find Tommy on the other side, his hand raised to knock. His jaw went slack for a moment before he grinned. "You're going in fully loaded, aren't you?"

"You bet." She smiled in return and spun. "What do you think?"

"I think you'll set half the men drooling in that outfit. With any luck all semblance of thought will fly right out of their heads."

"That is the plan. Now, may I pass?"

"Mind if we chat first?" He stepped into the room and off to the side. The option was hers. "I got some information on the children, and I'm expecting company."

Her heart sank at the mention of company. "Oh, well then. I suppose it's best if I leave."

"Would you close the door, woman? That isn't what I mean. Well, it is, but it isn't."

Some of the fire she'd had to confront Loren had deflated when Tommy suggested he'd invited a whore to the room. Still, she thought heading downstairs might be better than witness how her flirtations had backfired. Tommy was good as his word, though, so if he said it wasn't what he meant, maybe she'd best listen. With an indecisive shrug, she shut the door.

"Thank you." Tommy sat down with a sigh. "Which do you want first?"

Rather than seem too eager for an explanation for the whore he ordered, she took her own seat as slow and casual as she could. "What have you learned about the children?"

"All right, we'll start there. They are most likely the children of a family that lived about twenty miles from here."

"Most likely?"

"Around ten years ago when the attempted breakout from the reservation happened there were about three families with children at the right age based on what we guess those two to be." He leaned his elbows on his knees. "The other two families lived among the burned homes, and in both cases bodies of children were found, if not all the expected number of children."

"So we can't guarantee that those children weren't with those families?"

"One of the families all of the children were accounted for. The other, three weren't in the bodies found."

"And the family you first suggested?"

"They simply disappeared. All of them."

Leanne's heart sank. "Disappeared?"

"At first they thought the family gave up after the drought and left. With a little more searching they discovered the animals were still there, their wagon, and the crops were doing very well."

"So there was no reason for them to leave, much less without their supplies."

"Exactly."

Leanne frowned. "Do we have names? If we have a chance we can try to use them. The boy looks too young to remember, but perhaps the girl will remember."

"I do, and that is exactly what I'd planned to do." He smiled. "I thought you would be best to approach her. She seemed pretty nervous, but seemed to like you."

"She didn't even know me, but I'll do what I can. I'm not sure about the man that took her in. What do we know about him?"

"Jacob and Lucy have lost every child they've had. They struggled with babies dying, so they adopted. The child lived five years and fell out of a tree and died. They've been somewhat reclusive since."

Leanne's unease returned. "I don't wish to be a suspicious sort, but is it safe for the children to be there? I know no one else wanted to take them, but all things considered."

"That's why we are checking on them tomorrow. More if we need to. You aren't the only one that isn't entirely sure about the situation. I don't feel too good about it either. Unfortunately, there's not much you and I can do. This isn't our town and we aren't…"

"Appropriate guardians? Considering your sister and brother-in-law were no better than either of us when they took in their brood." Leanne laughed. "However, I concede your point. We are in a strange town. I'd suggest bringing Jane here, but that could be disastrous."

"She'd never come. She hates explaining that she doesn't remember anything from her past." Tommy rubbed his hands together. "Now, moving on. I'd like to ask you a favor."

"Is that so?" Leanne had the distinct impression the favor was nothing she'd want to hear.

"I know you're ready to go after Loren, and I understand why. I'd like to ask you to wait, though." He held up his hands at her attempt to protest. "Just a day or two until we have more information. That's why I paid for a whore—the one that told me about the banker. I'm betting I can get more information from her."

Leanne tightened her lips at the mention of the whore. "That's why you requested a girl?"

"For information only." He lifted his gaze to meet hers for the first time since his suggestion that she wait. "Wouldn't get a girl for myself after that kiss."

Despite her attempt to protest, a grin stretched its way across her features. "It was simply a kiss. Unless you wish it to be more, I won't push."

"My reverse Madam Bovary, I've always wished for more."

"Well, then." Her next words were cut off by a knock at the door. "I suppose it's too bad you ordered a whore."

"Leanne."

She ignored him to answer the door. A short, moderately pretty brunette on the other side lost her smile at the sight of Leanne. Leanne chuckled and glanced back toward Tommy. "I suppose I'll see you in an hour or two."

"Do we have an agreement?"

Leanne shrugged. She'd already decided to hold off, but after his poor handling of why he'd asked for a whore, she thought she'd toy with him a bit. "You'll have to wait and see."

* * * *

Tommy knew he had to not let Leanne's caginess distract him. The woman was out to drive him mad on this trip. She had been kidding when she left, of course. She'd wait as he'd asked her to. Right?

"Sir?" The whore stood in front of him, her brow puckered in confusion. "Ya paid for an hour, ya gonna stare at the door the whole time?"

"Right. Sorry." Tommy shook his head and rose. "I didn't pay for the usual."

"It's extra for anything else."

"For talking?"

"Oh." The confusion returned to her features, the smile fading. "It ain't a good idea. I should get going if that's what ya want."

"No, wait. I'll pay extra. Your boss doesn't ever have to know." He gestured toward the table. "Have a seat. Want some tea? Or whiskey?"

She moved back to the chair hesitantly. "I already told ya too much. I'm lucky Loren didn't hear. I figured ya just changed your mind about the offer."

"That was the plan." He poured himself some tea and set a cup by her in case she changed her mind. Once he'd sat down, he reached into his pocket and withdrew twenty dollars. He slid the money across the table. "There's more if you change your mind."

She stared at the money with wide eyes. "Boss'll know."

"I'm sure you have a stash. Every whore worth her salt has a stash hidden beyond what the boss knows." He nudged his chin forward. "Go on, take it. Even if you decide to not answer a thing, take an hour off on me."

A smile twitched across her lips. "It wouldn't be an hour off if I was on ya."

Tommy laughed. "Guess you have a point. Either way, take it. Have some tea. At least tell me your name."

"Enid." She snatched the money toward her as if afraid he'd take it back. Quick as a wink she had it stuffed in her corset. "Leastwise that's the name the orphanage gave me. Can remember my mama's face, can't remember the name she gave me for nothing."

"Orphanage, eh? Where was that?"

She seemed glad that the questions weren't about the twins or Loren. The tension around her pale green eyes eased, releasing the tiny wrinkles that had started to form. "Out east. New York City. Got put on an orphan train three times 'afore I was a teenager. Last time I was fifteen. Loren offered me a place, and I took it. Been here ever since."

"Can't have been, what, three years ago?"

"Six, actually." A pleased flush filled her cheeks. The compliment had the right effect and turned her tired, wan features around into the youthful glow he'd implied. She tucked a lock of dirty blond hair behind her ear. "Loren ain't so bad, but business has slowed."

"I imagine so. There's not much in the way of mining around here, and what silver there was near here went bust with the crash."

"We got a couple ranches outside town that bring in cowboys now and then, but they ain't exactly good business. They steal, and drink, and they use company, but aren't always good with the merchandise."

"Tell me about it." As Dominion Falls had begun to expand into ranching, they'd begun to have more problems with crime when the cowboys had arrived in town. Not only were they an outside element, they often clashed with the well-established miners in the town. It was an ugly mix they were still working on resolving. It was half the reason Cole had been scaring off any new brothel in town, that and he was trying to keep Leanne in business.

"Plus, that ain't steady none."

"So Loren's got to take his money where he can. Including letting guys rough you all up now and then. Does he rough you up?"

"Nah. He don't have to. Him being nice keeps us here, but he knows what he's got in Nellie and Flo. They bring in money, but they don't get treated good."

"How'd they hear about Leanne's place?"

"They saw the advertisement." Enid fidgeted in her seat, then grabbed the tea to pour it. "They can read real good. Been teaching some of the girls. They went to school when they were young. Guess their momma got killed in the Injun attacks, and soon as they were of age their daddy sold them off to Loren and skipped town."

"So they used their skills to send a few wires as if they were Loren." Tommy shook his head. "Not the best thought out plan I ever heard, but I guess desperation will do that to a person. I've seen it do worse."

"A couple of the girls weren't too happy, and word got out eventually." Enid sipped her tea quietly. "I didn't care either way. I don't mind it so much here, and I'm getting older so not so many bother with me no more. I got a regular pays me good."

He smiled when she patted her corset. "You've been saving up?"

"Contract is up in two years. Ain't sure what I'll do after that, but I plan on leaving Utah for sure." She finished her tea. "Not good for much, but I'll figure something out."

"I have no doubt you will. Thank you for all your help."

Her eyes widened in surprise. "I didn't do nothing."

"You gave me some idea into the how's and whys of Loren keeping those twins like he is. Not to mention how this business runs and the sort of clientele. It's all information I can use. Unless you want to clue me into any of Loren's weaknesses."

She chewed her lip, guilt lining her features again. "He likes his opium, every Monday he indulges since we're real slow on Mondays. That's how Nellie and Flo got to do all they did."

"Very good." Tommy went to pull out another twenty for her, then paused. He thought of her goal to get out in two years and wondered at what sort of limited amount she had put away. When he removed his wallet, he leafed through the bills and took eighty dollars out to make give her one hundred total. It was probably more money than she'd seen in her life.

His guess was proven right when she gasped and paled at the sight. She shook her head and held up her hands. "I couldn't."

"Do ya have somewhere real secure for your stash, Enid?"

"Secure as it can be 'round here."

He set down the eighty dollars on the table. "I wish we could help you out and take you as well as Nellie and Florence."

"Nah. I don't want a new contract. Two years ain't so bad." She couldn't tear her gaze off the money laid on the table.

"Then let me help you another way."

"Why?"

"Because you helped me today, and therefore, you helped Leanne." He leaned forward. "Plus, you seem pretty smart and put together. After all you've done and learned, I figure it's time for you to find something better."

"People don't do that. Not for nothing." Her hand trembled as she pushed the money back to him. "But thanks for pretending."

He frowned, but pulled the money closer. "Good thing I got another few days to convince you. I just want to help."

She rose, the money still her focus. "Well, I best get back downstairs." Her hands ruffled through her hair to muss it up. She fidgeted and fussed until her outfit was a bit askew.

"I'll be asking for you again. Tomorrow. Same time."

"Don't bother. I'm just trying to help my friends since they helped me learn to read. I done my part."

"But I haven't done mine yet."

Chapter 6

Tommy tucked the money away after Enid left. The woman had surprised him with her humor and strength in the position she was in. He'd seen it often in whores, but the girl had a plan, and he hoped he could help her see it through.

He rose, determined to seek out Leanne and finish their earlier discussion. Lucky for him he didn't have to go far. Or perhaps it was unfortunate for him. By the time he got downstairs, she was parked in the center of the saloon.

In one hand she held a half-finished glass of whiskey; in the other she had an entire crowd of men wrapped around her little finger. The tale she regaled them with was one familiar to him. The story of Jane's teasing of Cole on their trip to Denver, told with discretion back home, was being told whole hog now, nothing held back.

The men were salivating over the description of Jane's outfit, and what it had revealed. The whores lounging on and around the men held smiles of delight. Laughter both trickled and blasted at all the right times.

Leanne was in her element. He knew she could work a crowd, but at home she wasn't a new element any longer. Here she basked in the attentions, even the glowers of Loren. Her face lit with delight and amusement.

He'd be a fool if he let himself trip over his feet again. The matters he'd screwed up in the past were just that, the past. Besides, who knew if she even wanted a husband, or if she'd be content to remain as they were—if a hell of a lot closer.

When Leanne caught sight of him, she offered a wink before she returned to her story. Tommy went to the bar to allow her the stage to finish her tale. He nodded to Loren. "Whiskey and a beer."

Loren all but grunted in reply. When he set down the drinks he nudged his chin Leanne's direction. "You gonna get your woman in line?"

"I'm not stupid enough to do that." Tommy threw back the whiskey. He chased it down with a sip of beer before he bothered to speak again. "She lives to spin a tale. After all she's done and seen, she's got plenty of them. You should be happy. Men have whores, and are getting riled for more—and their tossing back the liquor faster than you can pour to whet their whistles."

Loren grunted another reply. Despite his protest, he poured another round for those around Leanne. "They ain't for sale, ya know."

"I'm not the one that cares. I just came as company. She's the one running the business." Tommy sipped slow on his beer while Loren delivered the drinks. By the time he got back, Tommy tapped his whiskey glass for another. "I got my own work."

"A woman ain't got a head for business," Loren protested.

Tommy snorted. "Don't say that to her or my sister back home. They'll knock you flat on your ass for it. I myself know at least ten women that have more business sense than most men. Leanne's at the top of that list. She was taught right how to run a brothel. Still makes damn good money in a town where most men can't afford her wares."

Loren grumbled a reply under his breath. While he wiped down the glasses and began to fill them again.

Tommy glanced over his shoulder to watch as Leanne launched into another story about some wealthy do-gooder that had first protested the brothel widely, only to become a regular patron. The tales of how he'd been seduced inside, along with his wife, were enough to make the most vulgar miner blush.

When he turned back to polish off his beer, he found another whiskey ready and waiting. He didn't hesitate to toss it down. "Anywhere to eat around here? We haven't eaten since we left the lodge this morning."

"Next to the mercantile." Loren focused on him. "What's your business anyhow?"

"A little bit of everything." Tommy spun his empty glass on the bar surface. "Deputy, hotel manager, among other things."

"It's the other things that I don't care none for."

"You and a lot of people." Tommy chuckled as he tossed back the last of his beer. The groans and complaints behind him led him to believe Leanne had finished her tale. He turned to find her heading his way. "You hungry after all that gabbing?"

"I think you know me better than that. I can talk the ears off a sow and keep going. However, my stomach is protesting our lack of sustenance." Leanne set her empty glass on the bar. "Thank you, Loren."

"I just asked where the grub could be found. Shall we?" Tommy held out his arm, happy to have her accept the offer.

Leanne walked silent until they'd left the saloon. Once out of sight of the doors, she leaned against him with more weight. "All those whiskeys were heading straight to my head on this empty stomach. It was all I could do to keep from tripping over my words."

Tommy chuckled. "That's what you get for trying to impress the idiot. He asked if I was going to get you in line."

"And you said?"

"That I'm not that stupid." He grinned at her laughter. "Between you, Jane, Kat and Lillian—I doubt there's many men left in Dominion Falls that are that stupid."

"Ah, but some will never change. Mack is still a bullheaded idiot of a man. Nearly having his neck stretched for stealing horses didn't even change him." She allowed him to hold the door for her. As they took a seat in the nearly empty restaurant, she leaned on the table. Her eyelids drooped in a clear sign of her level of intoxication. The woman could hold her liquor on a normal day, but between the exhaustion and hunger she was likely losing ground fast.

"We need to get you to bed."

"I'm happy to crawl into bed with you, but I need sustenance." A quiet gasp slipped from her lips. Though her eyes remained on the paper menu before her, a pleasant pink hue flooded her cheeks and seeped into her ears.

"I wouldn't mind that either, but I meant you need sleep."

"Of course."

Tommy groaned as the realization hit him. "Damn her all to hell and back."

"What?" Leanne lifted her head in surprise. "What the devil do you mean?"

"Jane. She was right."

"How?"

"She said if we got away from the town we'd relax and get back to it."

She pursed her lips. "Balls."

"She'll never let us live it down."

"We can't ever tell her."

"She's crafty. She'll find out." Tommy knew all too well how crafty she was.

"We're in trouble, then."

"Don't I know it?"

* * * *

Leanne was relieved to not wake with any more than a small headache the next morning. Drinking as much as she had on an empty stomach and tired mind hadn't been her smartest idea ever.

Still she'd made some leeway. If not with Loren himself, then with his girls and the men who made use of his saloon and women.

She had to admit a smidge of disappointment when she woke to find Tommy had not taken advantage of her light grasp on sobriety or her offer. He'd slept in the room, but on the floor.

After a light breakfast of tea and some trail crackers she'd been set to head out to the farm where the children had been taken. Unlike Tommy, she didn't find the sight of the wagon that would take them there amusing. After a couple of days in a stagecoach she'd rather ride a horse bareback than get into the rickety old wagon that appeared as though it might fall apart if all three of them got in.

Still, the elderly reverend couldn't ride, so they took the wagon. Each bump and lurch made her good night's sleep worthless. She would be quite happy when she got on the train and wouldn't have to worry about another wagon for some time.

When they finally pulled up to the small farm where the children were staying, her heart sank. All that sat on the land was a small house so run down there were boards falling off, a barn that could hardly house a cow and a horse, and a flew planks covering what she assumed was the well based on the bucket beside it.

There were no great crops, no fence for cattle or horse grazing. A small half-withered garden wilted in the burning sun.

She heaved a great sigh as they came to a stop. Tommy patted her hand as if he knew exactly what she was thinking. She rose from the seat and easily accepted Tommy's assistance down. While he assisted the reverend, she beat the dust from her skirts.

"There's Lucy," the reverend said quietly.

Leanne lifted her head in time to spot a pale face in the window the moment before it disappeared from sight. Jacob himself lounged on a cut log that served as a bench, puffing on a pipe. When he stood, he appeared none too happy with their appearance.

She accepted Tommy's proffered arm without hesitation. They headed toward the man glaring them down. She became keenly aware of the lack of laughter or any sound from the children. Nor did she see them anywhere.

"Jacob." The reverend spoke before she could, which was likely best or she might have regretted her words. "How are things with the children?"

"Fine. They're getting some milk. Doing chores as they should." He lifted his chin. "Ain't had no trouble. Got them in real clothes and everything."

Only the sharp squeeze to her hand from Tommy kept her mouth shut.

Tommy himself cleared his throat. "Don't you think it might have been better to let them ease into things? They were awful scared yesterday."

"No." Jacob narrowed his eyes at Tommy. "They gotta learn the right way to do things. Hard work will get the Injun out of them."

"May we see them?" Leanne kept her seething to herself well enough that Tommy didn't even cast her a sideways look at her request.

"They ain't yours."

"They aren't yours yet, either." Tommy's smile turned dark and threatening in a way she'd only seen a few men accomplish. "We just want to check on them. I have some doctoring knowledge and I want to see that they're not carrying any illnesses or injuries from their past."

Jacob didn't seem to have an argument, so he just shrugged. "They're this way."

Leanne followed, eager to see the children for herself. In no time they'd crossed the small yard to the barn. As the door opened, the children scattered from beside the cow to hide, which did nothing for Leanne's nerves.

She stepped around Jacob to enter the dimly lit space first. Keenly aware of the dark gaze at her back she approached the girl. A few feet away she knelt down. "Hello there. Remember me?"

The girl nodded once slow as molasses. Her brother crouched behind her, his gaze fixed on Jacob. Leanne noticed that the girl kept her hand fisted tight at her side.

Curious, Leanne held out her hand. "Would you come outside into the light? We'd like to see you again."

After some hesitation, the girl turned to her brother. They spoke low and quiet in the language they'd used the day before. They approached her together, hand in hand. When they got close enough, Leanne rose and set a hand on the girls shoulder.

Relieved she didn't pull away, Leanne guided the pair outside, being sure to put herself between them and Jacob as they passed. "There we are. Now let's see you two."

True to his word, Jacob had put the pair into white clothes. Ill-fitting and filthy ones, but definitely not what they'd been in. Both children were dirty, and the girl still kept her hand clutched close to herself.

Leanne glanced at Tommy. "Perhaps you men could get us some water. We'll see what we can't do to clean up these faces."

Tommy took the hint with a quick nod. He all but pushed Jacob back toward the house.

Leanne waited until they were some distance off before she turned back to the pair. "You poor things. You've been through it the past few days, haven't you? Now, what shall I call you? Do you have names?"

"Shivering Willow," the girl whispered. "He is Jaybird."

"You speak English." Leanne smiled in delight. "Wonderful."

"My parents spoke it. Let us speak both." Shivering Willow lifted her chin.

"Your parents? Were they with the Ute taken to the reservation?" At the girl's nod, Leanne sighed. "What are their names?"

Willow clammed up, shutting her mouth and shaking her head.

"All right. What about that? What do you have there?"

The girl's gaze darted toward where the men had disappeared. When there was no sign of them she held out her hand and opened. On her palm sat a shiny purple bead.

Leanne remembered the necklace around the girls neck the day before. "Did that come from your necklace?"

"He ripped it off." She nudged her chin toward the house. "I saved this."

"I see." Leanne frowned. "Is he mean?"

The girl closed her fist, and her mouth. In one quick motion she'd moved her brother behind her again. Pride and stubbornness took over her features.

"If he is, we can take you away somewhere."

The girl gave her a look filled with doubt. "Home."

"No, I can't do that." Leanne sighed. The voices of the men reached her ears. "Do me a favor. Find a place to hide that bead. Keep it safe. I'll see what we can't do to help you."

The girl tucked her hand behind her with her brother, chin lifted in a show of strength Leanne wasn't so sure she actually felt.

"I promise."

"White promise means nothing."

Chapter 7

Leanne finished washing off Shivering Willows face, and immediately regretted doing so. The young lady was a stunning beauty under the dirt and grime. The wild, untamed gleam in her eye only made her more so.

After years around men, Leanne didn't miss the way Jacob took new notice of the girl. She kept a careful eye on him as she worked on Jaybird's face as well. "I have learned their names."

"We believe we already know them." The reverend stepped closer. "And seeing this young lady, I'm more certain. She looks very much like her father. She's Josephine, and he is Louis. They're last name is Stephenson."

"*No*," the girl shrieked at the reverend. "Not—name. Not—parents. Not—anymore."

As her temper flared, her breath grew quicker, her cheeks flushed. After a few minutes the color drained from her face. She gasped for air, wheezing with every breath. Leanne flew to her side and so did her brother.

Jaybird raced back into the barn fast as lightning. Confused, Leanne tried to get the girl calm and breathing normally. When Jaybird came back outside he had a small bag clutched in his hand. Jacob tried to snatch it away, but the boy snarled and bit at the hand that reached toward him. He ran back to his sisters side.

Leanne watched quietly as he pulled open the bag and held it to her face. She turned to Tommy in confusion. Tommy knelt beside them. "Asthma, sounds like. He must have some kind of medicine in that bag."

After several long minutes Willow's breathing eased. She blinked slowly, then nodded to her brother and held the bag on her own. Leanne searched the girls face. "Better?"

Willow nodded, but didn't speak. Leanne pushed to her feet and turned to face the other two men. Jacob was still leering at the weakened young girl. "I think we shouldn't push them so much. They're young, scared, they've been ripped from what I believe they consider family."

Jacob snorted. "They're savages."

"To you and I, perhaps." Leanne frowned. "But they consider themselves one of them. They call themselves Shivering Willow and Jaybird."

"They'll go by Jo and Louis 'round here, and that's that." Jacob straightened. "I think it's time ya left now. They got chores to do."

"She needs time to recuperate." Tommy rose. "I'll hang around here for a while, help Jaybird with the chores. Why don't you take the reverend back to town, Leanne? Maybe send a telegram to Daisy. Let her know we got here safe and sound?"

Leanne smiled at Tommy's suggestion. "Good idea." She assumed he wanted her to let Daisy or Charlie know about the girls condition and get some advice. Although the boy seemed to have a handle on things, who knew how long that little bag would last—especially now that Jacob was aware of it.

Tommy nodded. "Maybe later we'll go for a ride out west of town. Take in the sights, if you're not opposed?"

She wasn't as sure about what he meant, but nodded none the less. He likely had his reasons. "I think that sounds lovely."

"Good." Tommy fixed a mean stare on Jacob as if expecting any objections.

Leanne bent closer to the young lady. "Shivering Willow."

Willow turned her tired features toward Leanne. Though she still wheezed some when she breathed, she lowered the bag.

"Remember what I told you." She stepped closer so she could whisper. "Protect what's precious. You're being very brave and strong. I know you don't believe me, but we're going to try to help."

Doubt still darkened her sharp eyes, but Willow nodded.

"Now rest up." Leanne raised her voice from the hushed tones. "We'll be back to check on you tomorrow."

Tommy nodded as she straightened. "I'll be fine to walk back. It's not that far. I'll see you in a few hours. Please behave while I'm gone."

"Well now you went and took all the fun out of it." She smiled as she spun on her heel. Without so much as a glance she bypassed Jacob. "Come, Reverend McGonagall. Let's get you back to town."

She helped the reverend back into the wagon and delivered him to his small home. Before she left, she thought of something else. "Reverend, does your town have a doctor to speak of?"

The reverend shook his head. "We had one, and his nurse is still here, but he had to return home to attend to a family emergency two years ago. Never did return."

"That's too bad. Thank you. Don't bother coming to us tomorrow. We'll pick you up around ten in the morning for a return trip. Will that work for you?"

"That would be fine. Thank you, Mrs. Young."

Leanne's cheeks grew warm at the implication, though she didn't dare contradict. She waved her goodbyes to head back into the heart of town. Once she'd returned the wagon to the livery, she set about sending the telegram. While there she pondered sending another to Jane to inquire with her about the children.

After a few minutes she thought better of it. Word would travel fast enough from Daisy to Charlie and then to Jane. Besides, as Tommy already pointed out, Jane would never come to Heber City. This was something they would need to handle on their own.

Honestly she wondered why they were handling it, but at the same time she didn't. Those children needed someone to make sure they were all right. She had someone to take care of her when her mother died, even if he did it in an unusual way, Cole had.

Those children needed the same. Especially since no one in this town seemed to care one way or another about them.

She sighed and shook her head to clear it.

First things first, she had to send her telegram.

Then she would wait for Tommy's return. Perhaps in the meantime she'd manage to at least catch sight of the twins. She couldn't forget her real reason for being here in all this chaos. She would have to start moving on Loren soon.

Last thing she wanted to do was end up stuck in Heber City for too long.

Even if things with Tommy were easier there where no one knew them.

* * * *

By the time Tommy got back to town he didn't feel much better about leaving the children at the farm, but at least Shivering Willow had regained her strength and seemed strong enough to withstand another night.

The girl was proud, and a fighter. Jaybird was quieter, but Tommy guessed that in a pinch the boy would fight tooth and nail. God willing, such a thing wouldn't be needed. Tommy didn't appreciate the way Jacob leered at the girl once she'd been cleaned up, though.

He hoped Leanne had got the telegram not only sent off, but had received a reply. The day before he'd been proactive enough to get a wire off to his buddy in Washington so they might visit the reservation to learn about the children. That meant they wouldn't have to wait another day. He hoped taking the kids a message from the parents they knew would help ease their panic, maybe loosen them up.

Leastwise he was pretty sure Leanne wouldn't vehemently oppose the plan the way his sister might. That would make the rest of the afternoon go somewhat smoother.

The path from Jacob's farm led him up to the back of the saloon they'd been staying in. When it came into sight his eye was immediately drawn to the long set of bare legs and barely covered rump hanging out of a window.

He drew close as the woman's feet hit the ground.

She waved at the window. "Come on, hurry up."

Tommy raised a curious brow when she turned to find him there. Her eyes widened as she reached for the leg that followed her out the window. When the head attached to the limb emerged, Tommy immediately understood. "Nellie and Flo, I presume?"

The girl in front of her opened and closed her mouth like a fish gasping for its last bit of air. In the window her identical twin flashed a smile. "I see our reputation precedes us."

"You could say that. What are you attempting to do here?" He had a good idea, but he figured he'd give them a chance to explain.

"Well, mister. It's simple." When the girl in the window spoke, her twin hushed her quickly.

"I'm here with Leanne DuBois, by the way. I know who you are, and I also know what tricks you pulled to get her here." Tommy smirked.

"I'm Flo." The girl still perched on the windowsill piped up. "So obviously this here is Nellie. How do we know you aren't lying?"

"You could be anyone." Nellie spoke quieter than her sister. Both their inflections were clean without rough speech. No wonder they were more prized. On top of the twin advantage, talking like a proper lady probably got the banker excitable.

Part of him wondered if it was his dead sister's influence carrying over. Then again, that was probably wishful thinking. Her time in these parts was a brief four years many years ago in the lives of these two.

"Maybe Loren sent you to check up on us." Nellie's eyes narrowed. "It doesn't help your case that you seem oddly familiar."

"We might have met once during your youth. My sister was your teacher years ago. That's what I'm guessing anyhow. I'm Tommy Young."

Flo almost fell out of the window in her rush. "Miss Clara? Whatever happened to her?"

"She died…in a manner of speaking."

While Minnie's head tilted at his turn of phrase, Flo didn't seem to notice. "We figured once she got married she just got all domesticated. Her husband stuck around forever, but we never saw her again."

"We didn't think that," Nellie corrected. "That's what our prick father said. She never even said goodbye. School wasn't the same after that."

"Neither was her husband's life, nor the lives of any of her brothers." Tommy nodded. "Some bad things happened to her. We lost her a long time ago."

"You said 'in a manner of speaking'." Nellie set her hands on her hips. "What's that mean?"

"That's a long story that I don't think you have time for now." Tommy checked the area for signs of life. "I imagine if you get caught, there'll be hell to pay."

"We don't care." Flo folded her arms across her chest. "We've got to get out of here. George is going to be here in a few hours for an appointment."

"You sound like intelligent women. Do you think trying to run off in a town where everyone knows you in the middle of the day is the smartest plan?"

"You don't understand." Nellie stepped closer. "We had a good plan, you just interrupted us. If you'll go about your day, we'll be gone and hidden well soon enough."

"And when you're found you'll be arrested." Tommy leaned against the back of the building. "I do understand, I heard about this George. I'll make you a deal."

"We aren't going back in there." Nellie shook her head.

"I can make sure he doesn't visit today. Leanne is working some sort of magic on Loren, it's just taking some time. Tomorrow is Sunday, George ever visit on Sunday?"

Flo shook her head. "He acts a good Christian on Sundays. You know, Sabbath and all that."

"Good. I don't want you two arrested or worse before we can work on this deal. I know Monday is the day Loren enjoys his opium."

"How'd you know that?" Nellie returned to suspicious.

"Enid." Tommy nodded when Nellie relaxed. "She likes you two, said you taught her to read and all, so she wanted to help you out. Plus, I gave her an hour off with pay, which helped."

"You really are trying to help us?" Nellie relaxed. "How are you going to keep George away? He's right-mad that we are trying to leave him. We can't have another day like Wednesday."

Tommy frowned when her hand went to her shawl-covered arm in what he thought wasn't a conscious action. "Don't worry about it. Just get back inside before someone sees you. We'll do what we can to get you signed to Leanne before George can make another move."

Flo went to help her sister back in the window. "Would you tell Miss DuBois we're real sorry for lying?"

"I'm guessing she already knows, but I'll tell her." He waited until they were ensconced back in the room with the window shut and locked before he moved again. By his estimations he only had about two hours before the last stage left for the week.

If he was lucky he could get George all the way out of town for several days and that was one less distraction in the mess of them he had on his plate.

He almost missed Leanne's approach in his rush to get the telegraph office.

"Tommy?" Leanne didn't try to get him to stop, rather she kept pace with him. "Where on earth are you going? You look as though you have a bee in your bonnet. Is it the children?"

"No, but yes, but no. I'm going to send a telegram."

"I already sent the telegrams."

"This is a new one."

"What? Why? Where? To whom?"

Tommy chuckled as he climbed the steps. "I'm sending it to a friend in Denver."

"You have friends everywhere." Her lips curved into a delectable smile, and he had the sudden urge to kiss her.

However, doing so would distract him from his task. Later, most definitely later he would kiss her, soundly. He shook his head from the distraction. "I do. I'm hoping this one will help keep those twins in place until you can work one over on Loren."

"How so?"

"Give me five minutes and I'll explain."

"I hate it when you say that."

Chapter 8

Tommy explained to the telegraph operator what he needed done. His telegram would go to his friend in Denver that was handling all the paperwork for his false-front of an investment company. The man would likely get back within fifteen minutes. He kept a telegraph in his house, Tommy paid him well enough to do so.

Leanne remained silent, but well attentive as he worked, then followed him outside. "What was that about?"

"Let's have a seat for a bit, shall we? I'd like to see if my plan works."

"Thomas."

"There's two things men like this George character respond to. Money and women—but mostly money. He doesn't care much about the human element, he just likes to abuse it."

Leanne sighed as he led them a fair distance from the telegraph office. It wouldn't do to be too obvious when the banker arrived. She didn't speak until he'd stopped them near the creek. As she did, she knelt to pluck some flowers. "You aren't telling me anything I don't already know. I meant what was that telegram about?"

"You heard it. I simply told my friend to imply we had enough to tear down his bank based on his shady business practices."

"And do you?"

"No, but I can and will. Man like that probably doesn't do well with other people's money. He's probably even lied to the bank headquarters in Salt Lake about what he's doing." Tommy knew that this bank here was a division of a larger one in Salt Lake. The town didn't warrant its own budding bank. "His panicked run to get his ducks in a row should give me time to get all the dirt through some sources."

Leanne eyed him quietly. "All right."

"I promised Nellie and Flo I'd get him out of town before they went and did something stupid like try to run away in broad daylight."

"Wait, you saw them?" She scooted closer. "When? How?"

"Just now on my way back from seeing the children."

"What are they like? How are the children? Will the twins do? Is Willow all right? Oh, dear. I can't decide."

He set her hand on his, keeping his laughter in check as it would fluster her more. "First, when I left Shivering Willow was doing much better. She'd secreted away her medicine again and Jaybird was caring for her."

"I don't care for the way Jacob was taking notice once I cleaned all the filth off her face." Leanne shuddered. "I know that look and it isn't good."

"That's why we're going to keep an eye on things. They're pretty fierce children. Don't think he'll get anywhere if he tries. In the meantime we'll head to the reservation this afternoon and see if we can't find the people that raised them."

"We're going to do what?" She focused on him for a long minute. "Are you sure we'll be able to get in there. I imagine the army isn't too eager to let anyone on there to see whatever they do. Plus, Willow wasn't too keen on giving me her parents' names. Maybe she thought we'd do something to them or something, I'm not sure."

"She probably was trying to protect them." He frowned. "Speaking of. Before we move onto the twins—did you hear back from Daisy?"

"Yes." Leanne bit her lip. "I must have gone into too much detail, or it was the mention of a lack of a doctor here, but she said she's getting on the next train. I tried to discourage her, but she would have none of it."

Tommy didn't know if it was a bad idea or an excellent one. "And she said she was coming, not Charlie?"

"At first she said it would be one of them, but at the end of our exchange it was clear it would be her."

"Good. I'd rather her than Charlie if one of them is coming. Charlie would get too high and mighty over what was the right thing to do. I'm less likely to argue with Daisy."

"You aren't being soft because she's a woman?"

"Hell no. I just prefer working with women. They're skin is softer and their language sharper. Plus, I like a challenge."

Leanne grinned broadly at his statement. "You can be such a charmer."

"I know." He leaned closer, but paused as the telegraph operator emerged from the office across the way. "Well, let's wait and see what happens now, shall we?"

"Do you really think it will work?" Leanne crept closer. "What if the operator spills the beans? Or if George is smarter than you give him credit for and sees through the ruse?"

"Very few men ignore a message from a Pinkerton that contains threats, my dear." He winked at her. "And as for the operator—I think he'll abide by his oath. I don't think he cares enough for George for it to matter to him what happens. Who knows, maybe he's vindictive. If I remember right, that man was the owner of the mercantile and a small mine back when

Clara taught here. I imagine the silver crash wasn't too good on him or his accounts."

"You and your sister and your minds." She tapped his temple. "It is odd."

"At least we can't accuse Nick of the same thing. He's smart as a whip, but his memory for detail isn't all that long. He has to go back and look at his notes."

She shook her head at his chortling. "Siblings."

"Look at your sibling."

"I know. Sometimes I think it's far easier that we don't acknowledge that relationship. We aren't required to bicker for the sake of bickering or pick for the sake of teasing. He's still protective and watchful, but not smothering because he can't be without revealing his secret."

"Sometimes, but not always."

She shrugged, her gaze off down the street. "What about—oh, wait. There they are. That man does not look at all pleased."

"Good. Let's see that he stays that way, and is on the stage that's due here in a couple hours."

* * * *

They had both agreed that to sit around where they were would seem too suspicious. Since they had a little time they ate some lunch, then Tommy disappeared on Leanne only to show up ten minutes later with some fishing poles and a basket.

She shrugged as she took one from him. "I'm not much of a fisherwoman, but sounds like a plan. Will we have enough time to head to the reservation after all of this?"

"I'm sure we will. We might return after dark, but we shouldn't have any issues." Tommy led her back to the creek near the telegraph office. Not so close to be obvious, but close enough to see the stagecoach clearly. "I'll get some worms."

"I'll help. I don't mind getting my hands dirty." She hiked her skirts so she could drop close to the ground to dig.

"Wait. No need to get your hands that dirty." He withdrew a wooden stake along with a metal rod from the basket. "We'll get them the easy way."

Leanne eyed him in confusion. "What on earth?"

"You've never seen anyone get worms out of the ground?"

"Short of digging, no. I told you I'm not much of a fisherwoman so I never paid much attention to how to get worms out of the ground. I much rather they stay where they were."

He chuckled as he pounded the stake into the ground. "Keep an eye out, they'll show up soon enough." Without another word he began to run the metal along the stake. An odd grunting noise filled the air.

Right when it all began to get ridiculous and she was about to yell at him for teasing her, she spotted a worm wriggling along the ground. Then another joined it. She gasped and grabbed the small bowl he'd set out. Within five minutes the bowl was half full and he'd pulled the stake from the ground. She settled back on the ground. "That was delightfully easy."

"Exactly." He set about getting the poles together for fishing. She didn't argue when he set the worm on the hook for her. Though she didn't mind getting a little dirty, the thought of stabbing a worm onto a hook wasn't her favorite.

"Now that we're settled will you tell me about the twins? You said you saw them."

Tommy handed off her pole and started on his own. "I did. They were trying to sneak out of the brothel in the middle of the day like no one would see them."

She frowned. "That doesn't sound too intelligent."

"I think they're plenty smart, it was more desperation. They had a scheduled appointment with George, the banker. I guess they figured we were a lost cause."

"We've only been in town for a day." She sighed. "Then again, when you're desperate time does seem interminable, I suppose."

"That's about what I was figuring." He set his own hook in the water a few feet from hers. "Flo seems like the impulsive one. Nellie really seems to take time and think on things."

"Will they fit in well at my sort of brothel?" She did hate to be superficial, but her whores had to maintain a certain level of appearance. The unique call of twins would only go so far if they didn't have a certain look.

"From what I saw, they'll fit in nicely. They're intelligent, so they could carry on proper conversation probably with very little training."

"A definite plus." She pondered quietly as she watched her stagnant fishing line. "Now the challenge is getting them away from Loren. He's greedy enough, but I don't think he's interested in what any of his girls offer."

He shot her a sideways glance. "You caught up on that?"

"Please. I may not know what it's like to lie with a man via firsthand knowledge, but I know how to read men. He didn't even give me a once over. None of his girls buddy up to him, and I doubt he uses any of their services. Either he can't, or he's not interested in women."

"I got the same impression." He turned back to his fishing as his line twitched. "I haven't spent enough time in the saloon itself to figure out which it is, though."

"Neither have I. You said he indulges on Mondays?"

"That's what Enid said."

"Then we'll have to spend a little time around the saloon tomorrow. See what we see." She popped open the basket he'd brought, not surprised to see a couple of apples inside. As she wiped one off, she pondered. "Then perhaps a little money and coercion will be required."

"I've got the coercion down."

"I've noticed." She chuckled. "I don't think there's a man in Dominion Falls that isn't aware of that. We'll just have to make sure this one is."

"I also brought some money with me in case you think you won't have enough."

"I'm not worried." Without Jane's help that was one thing she'd managed quite well. She had a nice stash stored away in her luggage, hidden discreetly in unlikely places. With any luck she wouldn't require it all. "Though I appreciate you thinking that far in advance."

"I'm here to help."

"And to make sure this isn't more than an odd coincidence that Jane once resided here."

"I dismissed that pretty early. Soon as I realized those girls had gone right under Loren's nose I knew it was nothing more than coincidence. Clara was here so long ago most people have moved on. The twins remember her, though. She was their teacher."

"That will make for an awkward reunion. I should probably forewarn her."

"Just don't mention the children." He took a bite of his own apple. "Not until we know more. Not that I think it would matter. She wouldn't want to take them in any more than any person in this town does."

"You underestimate her, and the gossip in town. I'd wager a bet that she already knows about the children. Daisy and Charlie know."

"Good point."

She took a bite of her own apple. The juicy sweetness distracted her for a few minutes. Once she'd regained focus, she frowned. "Either way, we can't leave them here. They'll end up in an orphanage. Back in Dominion Falls maybe we can find someone. You said they had no family left to speak of, didn't you?"

"According to Reverend McGonagall, they are all gone."

"Then it's either take them home or leave them at the reservation with the parents they've always known."

"Where they'll be treated as poorly as the Indians there?"

Her appetite faded at the disgusted tone in his voice. "I've never been to a reservation. Is it really that bad?"

"It's worse."

"Oh."

"There's the stage." Tommy pulled his line from the water to reveal a fish. He freed the fish and tossed it back into the water. "And there's our guy—with a suitcase."

"Good. One less wrinkle to face."

"The biggest one remaining is getting everything done before he returns. That includes dealing with the children—

and we have to wait for Daisy to make sure the girl is well enough."

"If he's going all the way to Denver we have the time. Right?"

He nodded. "Barring he doesn't gather some brains on the journey and turn back."

"Brains, or cowardice."

"Either-or."

Chapter 9

Leanne dropped any pretense of banter when they got close to the reservation. She noticed the mood of the man beside her also changed. Something about the desolate area they'd put the camp reeked of dreariness.

The closer they got, the more her mood sank. The only bright spot was the hint of chatter they could hear from the area. The little notes of cheerfulness made her think that perhaps hope hadn't completely left the place.

Tommy pulled to a stop in front of the gate. As planned, he hopped out without a word to deal with gaining entrance. He had arranged for their entrance through another one of his mysterious and powerful friends.

She made to disembark, only to allow her foot to slip on the wagon wheel. Her stumble drew the attention of many of the soldiers away from Tommy's conversation with the sergeant in charge. They scrambled to assist her down from the wagon.

Without hesitation she accepted the offers and turned on the charm. Each man got a compliment in turn, a smile and a wink. By the time Tommy arrived to escort her in, he had to fend them all off.

He chuckled low as they approached the entrance. "Thank you."

"I figured if there weren't some sort of show of dominance with his men keeping such watch, you might have an easier time." Leanne shrugged. "So I did what I do."

"That isn't all you do. Not for me, anyhow."

"Well, you are special, Mr. Young." She winked. "Do we have word on who the parents might be or is this a search mission."

"It's a search mission." Tommy squeezed her hand. "Though it might be faster to separate, given the circumstances I think it's best we stick together. You won't argue, will you?"

"Not a whisper." In this particular case, Leanne knew better than to argue the point. Though men were men wherever you went, there was an air of anger and suspicion about the people that had seen them already. "I admit I will readily bow to your people skills in this situation. This environment is not one I am comfortable manipulating."

Tommy set his hand at the small of her back as they started walking. Anytime someone met his gaze he asked if they knew where Shivering Willow and Jaybird's parents were. Some clearly didn't understand English, others flat-out turned their backs on them, but neither of them missed how a few people took notice.

Leanne wondered how fast word would travel in a camp this small, and wasn't overly surprised when within ten minutes a couple rose to face them rather than ignore them. The pair kept their chins raised proud, but a myriad of emotions colored the woman's eyes.

Tommy nodded to them. "You are the parents of Shivering Willow and Jaybird? She said you spoke English, I hope that's true. I'm afraid my Ute is rusty."

The man glanced around for soldiers, then nodded once slowly.

"Are they well?" Though her voice was low, it was strong with no hint of the tears that lingered in her eyes.

"Yes." Leanne smiled at the woman's relief. "We are doing what we can to help them, but we are strangers here."

"You are from far away?" The man sought them both out in turn. "Who has them?"

"A couple from outside town. We're watching the situation." Tommy's frown remained in place, his displeasure for the situation clear. "We have a doctor coming in to check on Shivering Willow. She had an attack this morning, I assume you know what I mean?"

"She had a medicine bag. Did they take it?" The woman clutched her husband's arm.

"Jaybird hid it and used it to help her this morning. We only fear that now that it's been seen it will be taken. That's why we asked our friend to come and help."

The woman sighed. "They have nowhere now. We protected them as we could."

Leanne stepped a little closer. "How did you come to raise them? I'm sorry, I don't even know your names."

The couple stared at each other for a long moment before he gave a small, subtle nod. The woman turned back to them. "In your language, I am White Fawn. He is Eagle Eye."

"I am Leanne, this is Tommy. It's good to meet you. The children were clearly happy in your care. Shivering Willow became upset when it was suggested they take back their original white man names." Leanne was glad to see White Fawn smile in response. "I'm sorry this happened to you, and to them."

"You are one of the few who would be." Eagle Eye frowned. "We found them, alone and near starving. We believe another tribe took the rest. The father was dead with a

Navajo arrow. The girl has her sickness, I think they left her for dead. I cannot be sure. It was many years ago."

Tommy cleared his throat and shook his head. "You did a good thing. If we could return them to you, we would."

"Do not. Not here. They do not belong here." White Fawn's tone cracked in desperation. "They would not be safe here."

"I don't know how safe they are out there, either." Tommy glanced at Leanne. "They trust no one, and I don't blame them. Did you know they were from here?"

"No. We were many miles from here, traveling to a new camp. When she was well enough to talk, Shivering Willow did little to speak of her life before. We had no children of our own, we were happy to take care of them. They became our children." Eagle Eye put his arm around his wife when she lost brief control of her tears. "We cannot care for them here. It is not safe."

Leanne's emotions choked away her ability to speak for a moment. She forced back the tears. "I promise to do whatever I can to find them somewhere safe. Somewhere they will not be pushed to forget you."

Tommy's gentle touch to her back changed as he slid his arm around her waist and held her gently. He didn't balk at her words. "I will make the same promise."

"They are not welcome in this town. Not as they are." Eagle Eye shook his head. "You said you came from far."

"They aren't much kinder to your kind there, either." Tommy frowned and met Leanne's gaze. "But there are a few that are sympathetic. If we must take them away to make sure they remain safe, and don't end up in an orphanage, we'll do what needs done."

"We only wish them to be safe, and happy." White Fawn's hand trembled and she reached hesitantly toward Leanne. "We can no longer provide this."

Leanne didn't hesitate to clasp the woman's hand. She knew that Tommy, though hesitant before was in this situation right along with her. "We will do all we can. I don't know how, but we'll find a way."

"Thank you." White Fawn released her hand as quick as they'd grabbed it. Soldiers drew close, and the woman remained silent until long after they'd passed.

Tommy did the same, eying the departing soldiers with a cold eye. "I might be able to help you get to a better place, too."

"There is no place better alongside the white man." Eagle Eye's gaze darkened. "Make sure Shivering Willow and Jaybird are safe, and we will live on in them."

Leanne lowered her gaze at his refusal of assistance. Rather than argue, an action she was certain Tommy would object to right then, she took a deep breath. "Have you a message or anything you would like send to the children?"

White Fawn disappeared into the ramshackle hut they'd been situated in. When she emerged she held two small beaded pieces of leather. "We were forced to give up most everything. I managed to save a few things. These are for them."

Leanne accepted them, but immediately slipped them to Tommy so they might be hidden. "We will see they get them."

"Thank you." As the soldiers approached again on another sweep, she nodded. "You should go now. Before more trouble comes."

Tommy led Leanne away without so much as a nod to the couple. They were in the wagon and driving away before he broke the seemingly unbreakable silence. "I'm still gonna help get those two moved. Our presence probably made a bad situation worse."

"Please do. I wish we could emancipate them like Black Moon back home."

"That would be a long shot, but a more lenient reservation I could do."

"Is there such a thing?"

"Sometimes."

* * * *

Tommy always had a plan. They didn't work every time, but that's what backup plans were for. He hadn't quite worked out the logistics yet, but he knew the children wouldn't be staying at the farm of Jacob. That had to be nothing more than a temporary solution. He hoped they could convince the reverend to allow them to take them home. Problem would be when they also left with the twins.

Of course, that happened to be another problem they had to deal with. The sooner, the better even. He hoped that on Monday when Loren indulged in his recreation they'd be able to get a good span of time for Leanne to meet them.

Granted, they were supposed to already be on a train home, but apparently life had other plans. For now he'd run with what they had to get done. Since little could be done that night, what with it being the busiest night in most saloons, perhaps he and Leanne could get a little alone time as well.

They dropped the horses at the livery. Before they'd made it halfway to the saloon, the telegraph operator flagged him down. Rather than go on ahead, Leanne waited for him.

He imagined she was curious, and she'd have been right to be so. The telegram turned out to be from Jane herself. He sighed as he read the note.

"What is it?" Leanne approached after he'd paid the man. "Bad news?"

"Depends on how you look at it. It's from Jane."

"Really?"

"I don't want to tell you." Tommy folded the telegram in half. "I don't like a gloating woman. It gets under the skin."

"Gloating?" She grinned at the mere implication. Already she knew she'd been right. "Tell me. I'll get it out of you one way or another, and you know it."

"Fine. She says this." He opened the telegram. "Daisy told me all. You should have told me direct. How are the children? Tell me more about them. No promises. Don't get hopes up."

"So she's asking after them." Leanne preened. "That's a step."

"Don't go running away with yourself, there." He cupped her elbow to hold her still. "You think this town is bad with it's Indian-hating, it doesn't have anything on Jane. She carried that hate over from Clara, through the depths of her amnesia."

"Not to mention she was shot by the Renegades, and Cole's business was blown to bits. I know all of this." She didn't pull away, but set her hand on his chest. "But she asked. That's more than you expected, isn't it?"

He offered a begrudged nod. "It is."

"Then why not take it as a good sign?"

"Because I know Jane. She won't get over this. She has distance now."

Leanne frowned.

"There aren't a whole lot of people in Dominion Falls that are any more tolerant than those here. Not after the Renegade attacks back when Jane first got there." Tommy tucked a finger under her chin. "I just don't want you getting your hopes up too soon."

"What about David? He's friends with Black Moon, or Cora?"

"Cora's about done raising her boys, I don't think she would want a new challenge being all by herself like she is. David is fresh married with a baby on the way." He smiled. "You've been thinking about this long and hard."

"I just don't like the way Jacob looked at her. I don't think anything is right about where they are. I have such a bad feeling. I don't even know how we'd take them away being what we are here, which is nothing but a whore and her companion."

"I thought you knew by now."

"What?"

"When it comes to us Young's, we always find a way." He winked. "Now let's get back to the saloon. Not much else to be done today but to see what else we can get done about your twins. You up for some fun?"

"Always." She pushed forward a smile bright enough to almost fool him. He could tell that underneath the sunny smile she was still worried for the children. "Hey, speaking of fun. What do you think about going to church in the morning?"

"Interesting." He tucked her hand in his elbow as they headed to the saloon. "Are you encouraging Reverend McGonagall's belief we are married, while knowing half the town is suspicious?"

"Perhaps. Besides, it will be good to see if Jacob actually shows up, or Lucy, or the children. If they aren't, that'll make it easier to pick up the reverend to go out and see them."

"Smart thinking, if a little devious."

"Plus at home I don't get strange looks at church, Reverend Greene wouldn't ever allow it. Here it might be a giggle to see some reactions. I highly doubt they've ever seen a whore in church, no matter her sexual status."

Tommy chuckled. "You are a wicked woman."

"Life would be awful dull if I wasn't."

"You're telling me." At the door he paused. "Are you going in as is, or do you need a change? You seemed more ready when you were all gussied up."

"I already broke the tension." She fluffed a few curls along her lunatic fringe. "I think I'm ready without all the bells and whistles."

His reply was cut off when she bumped his hip with hers and strode into the saloon with her skirts swinging. There wasn't a minute that passed before the relative quiet inside erupted into laughter. He shook his head and followed her in to find her perched on the filthy bar, skirts to her knees.

If he were a better man, or maybe a less sexually deprived, he might have looked away. As it stood he did not avoid scanning inch of her exposed ankles, calves, and knees. Granted, he'd seen more when she changed in his company, but he still couldn't look away.

Maybe it was the way she'd so desperately cared about what happened to the children. Maybe it was the peace and quiet they had without prying eyes, but damn if he didn't feel more strongly attracted to her than ever before.

Then the thought returned to his head. *Virgin*. He took a shaky breath and blew it out long enough to kill the panic that had settled in. Damn it, he was caught between a rock and a hard place. If he didn't act soon, maybe someone else would. Or maybe she'd start actually using her position as madam.

No, he couldn't have that.

All he had to do was stop being a coward.

Chapter 10

Tommy had to give it to Leanne. She sat cool and quiet on the bench beside him in church. Her sweet voice joined the others in hymns and prayer without hesitation. Back home she attended church regularly, but here no one knew that she wasn't truly a whore. Which meant glances and whispers and likely harsh words and gossip even under the sanctuary of the church.

When the service ended, she remained in her seat. Tommy didn't argue, only sat beside her quietly while she leafed through the bible in silence. Once only a few of the townsfolk were left to leave the church, he leaned close. "You all right?"

"Certainly. A person doesn't become a madam, or a best friend to Jane Spencer, without growing accustomed to idle gossip." She gave him a sideways glance. "I just figured it was best to leave Reverend McGonagall to tend to his flock and their harsh or suspicious words as he sees fit."

"Ah. And if he decides to no longer accompany us out to the farm?"

"Then there is one less person on our side, though I believe he'll remain on the children's side. I wonder if we shouldn't have contacted Nick to see the legal ramifications and steps."

"He'll probably tell you what Jacob would." Tommy knew his tone was unreasonably harsh, but he couldn't tame the flare of jealousy over the mention of his brother. "They're children. They have no rights."

"I doubt anyone in the Young family would say such a thing. What put a bee in your bonnet?"

"Nothing."

She tsked. "Lying in church. Shameful."

The door to the church opened again, and the shuffling footsteps led him to believe the reverend had re-entered the church. He turned to find himself right. "Reverend McGonagall."

"Lucy was not at church again today." McGonagall took a seat on the bench in front of them. "You saw her the other day too, didn't you?"

"I-I saw someone in the window. I can't attest to who it was." Leanne set down her bible. "Seeing as I have never met her, that is."

"Oh, that was her." McGonagall clapped his hands to his knees. "Shall we? I'd like to see if I might check on Lucy this time."

"Oh. Well, certainly." Leanne rose.

"You seem surprised." McGonagall accepted her offered arm and assistance into the aisle. "Mrs. Young, my flock's words are just that. I am old, but not blind. I call you as I do because you and your friend failed to give me your name. Also, it stirs doubt for their own gossip in those around you."

Tommy grinned as he followed them toward the door. "That is almost wicked, Reverend."

"I prefer to call it enlightening."

Leanne's laughter was soft and carried on the wind when they stepped outside. "Well, thank you. I admit I was a little concerned, as was Tommy I believe."

"Whatever you may or may not be, you genuinely care what happens to those children. That's what matters." McGonagall let Tommy help him into the wagon. He grew silent while Tommy helped Leanne into the wagon as well.

Tommy climbed in behind them both. Situated next to Leanne he caught the reverend eying them both. Rather than ask what he found interesting, Tommy turned his attention to the horses. "I've seen a lot of wrong in my life, done a few wrong things, too. When there's a chance to do right, I take it. They're just kids. There's no law protecting them, so someone has to."

"They've already lost the only parents they remember." Leanne sighed. "It's tough losing your only family that way. If you've got no one to help, it's even worse."

"Sounds like you're speaking from experience." The reverend settled back.

"I am. Someone helped make sure I was taken care of. There seems to be no one around here besides you that really cares what happens to them." Leanne frowned. "I don't think Jacob does much, either."

Tommy couldn't help but think of the way Jacob had eyed the young girl the day before once Leanne had cleaned the children up. He urged the horses on quicker, worried that maybe he did care what happened to Willow, just in the wrong way.

Right outside of town Tommy noticed birds circling in the skies in the same direction as they were going. By his calculations the birds were close to their destination. Though he knew the odds were he could be wrong, he slapped the reins to pick up the pace further.

The wagon jerked forward hard enough to make Leanne yelp. She frowned his way, but at his nod followed the direction of his gaze. She frowned and shook her head. "Too far."

"I hope you're right." He could tell his foot pressed into the front of the wagon like it would move them faster. When they finally drew close to the farm, his heart sank. The birds circled and swooped right overhead.

The door to the small house stood wide open. Halfway between the home and barn was a pile of what appeared to be clothes. Tommy's stomach turned at what they could be facing.

Leanne gripped his wrist so tight her nails dug into his flesh. "Dear heavens, what is that?"

"I don't know for sure yet." He had a sneaking suspicion, but he didn't dare say it aloud just yet. He pulled the wagon to a stop. "Both of you stay here. I'm going to check everything out."

The death grip Leanne had on his arm released. Her wide, icy blue eyes focused on the barn. "The children. Tommy."

"Stay here." He said it more firmly, his gaze fixed on her. "If I say so, you take the reverend and go back to town for whatever law you can find. You hear me?"

Leanne's head bobbed in a slow nod.

"Take the reins now. Please, Leanne. I need to see what's what here. I need to know you're ready to go if I say it."

In slow motion, Leanne did as she was told. She opened her mouth, then appeared to think better of it and clamped it shut. After a minute, she turned to face him. "Don't get killed and find those children."

"I'll do my best on both accounts."

* * * *

Leanne gripped the reins tight so she wouldn't fidget and accidentally startle the horses into motion. Beside her Reverend McGonagall prayed in soft tones.

Though she wanted little more than to run to the barn to check the children, she remained in the wagon as instructed to by Tommy. She held her silence as he pulled his weapon free before he checked the lump of fabric on the ground.

With slow and steady breaths she tamed her nerves best as she could. Every second he spent checking the house and then the barn rattled her nerves more. When he finally emerged without the children her heart broke.

At his wave she clicked her tongue to urge the horses forward. They responded with a slow roll toward the homestead. "The children?"

"Can't find them. Both Jacob and Lucy are dead." Tommy helped the reverend down. "They've both been beaten and shot, it seems."

"Heavens!" Leanne ran toward the barn without another word. The children might hide from him, she hoped that if they were, they'd emerge when she showed up.

Inside the barn she called for them and checked both stalls before ascending the ladder to the small loft. By the time she got back outside, Tommy's brow was furrowed in concern. She took a shaky breath. "We have to find them."

"I agree. We have to make sure they're safe, and find out what happened here. It makes no sense." He knelt down next to Lucy. With the reverend inside the house, he spoke in low tones. "Tell me what you notice."

Leanne hesitated to look down at the woman, but did as he asked. She lowered herself to Tommy's level and spoke as quiet. "Some of these bruises on her face are old. She's thin as a rail. What happened to her?"

"Best guess is he's been beating her, that's why she stopped going to church. He's only got some wounds on his head that are recent. I saw a skillet in the barn." Tommy met her gaze. "We shouldn't leave the reverend alone here. We have no idea what happened. They've both been shot, but I didn't find Jacob's gun on him."

"But the children."

Reverend McGonagall drew close. "You should both go find them. I'll be all right here."

Tommy rose. "We don't know what happened. It might not be safe."

"I'll be fine. The children should be found. They could be in danger, and are at the very least frightened." McGonagall waved off Leanne's protest. "If it takes too long, we'll take the bodies back and the two of you can go out on horseback to search."

Leanne met Tommy's gaze. With any luck the children were only hiding, if they weren't a small search of the area could resolve the whole situation. "Can we take two hours and search?"

Tommy's gaze swept across the area, before it fell back on the barn. "Two hours. Let's get Lucy inside away from the buzzards. Are you sure you'll be all right, reverend?"

"I've been in worse fixes. Go do what needs done, I'll be here when you get back." McGonagall led the way back to the house when Tommy stooped to pick up Lucy's body.

Leanne lingered behind, searching the area for what would be the best hiding place. A line of brush about an acre away indicated a creek bed at the least. For children, even that small amount of brush would supply ample coverage. Off in the distance she could see a grove of trees.

Tommy emerged a few minutes later. He lifted his hat to scratch the top of his head. "Let's check for a trail behind the barn."

"Of course." Leanne was no dunce. She knew Tommy had once been a Pinkerton and could track a man across miles of prairie, she'd heard the tales. If the children had taken off, they'd may have left a bigger trail, or a smaller one depending on how much they'd learned in their life with the Ute. "What about the creek?"

"The girl's got good sense, and raised by the Ute—that's probably where they headed. I'm guessing they used that door in the back of the barn. It's not locked anymore, and it was the other day." Tommy circled the barn, not complaining when Leanne stuck close to him.

She used care to not move ahead of him wherever he looked, but kept her gaze in the distance. It was only a few minutes before he appeared to find a trail, but it seemed like hours. She wasn't sure if she should disturb him, so she bit her tongue.

They made their way to the creek, but a few yards down, Tommy jumped the narrow band of water. He knelt low. "They crossed here. Can you make it across?"

She didn't even bother to lift her skirts. "Water be damned, we need to find them. Which way?" She pulled herself up the steep bank, and was relieved for the boost he gave via a firm push to her rear.

"They were scrambling up that embankment. I think after this they'll be harder to follow. We'll do our best, though." Tommy pulled himself up beside her. "Your dress is muddy."

"It'll survive or it won't." She walked alongside him, pausing when he did. "What about that copse of trees over there?"

"Not enough places to hide. If they're on their own, and it seems that way, they'd look for somewhere they could hide." He took her hand in his and gave a squeeze of comfort. "All signs point to them being alone. We just need to look. You might call for them. The girl really seemed to take to you."

For nearly half an hour they searched, alternating between Leanne calling for the children and Tommy pausing to search for signs of a trail. Right when it seemed like they might need to turn back they both paused at the top of a small hill. In the distance they could see the remnants of dead mines with a nearby ramshackle shed that had once been the office. Skeletons of tents dotted the land, a dreary reminder of what the silver crash had done to many mining sites.

Leanne's stomach churned. "You don't think they went in a mine, do you?"

"I hope not. We might never find them if they did." He released her hand so they could make their way down the hill into the abandoned camp.

"Shivering Willow? Jaybird? Are you here? Please come out. It's Leanne and Tommy. You're safe now, I promise. We just need to find you!" Silence echoed back to her initial call, save for a weak echo through the small valley.

"Keep calling. You all right if we separate? Don't go too far, I want you in my sights, but we can search this camp better if we work separate."

“I’ll be fine.”

“Stay in my sight.”

“You stay in mine, too.”

Chapter 11

The more they searched, the more Leanne's heart sank. They were getting too close to the abandoned mines. If the children were in there, they might never find them.

She called again for the children, expecting once again to get no response. Instead, over the rattle of a stone she accidentally kicked, she heard another quiet noise. Almost a whimper, or perhaps a whisper.

"Shivering Willow? Jaybird? Is that you?" She spun in a circle trying to determine the source. The odd echoes of the area made determining the right course to take difficult.

"Leanne? You got something?" Tommy made his way around a tent skeleton.

"I thought I heard something. I have no idea where it came from, though. Jaybird? Shivering Willow? Please come out. It's Leanne and Tommy. We're alone." This time she remained still, and was relieved to find Tommy did the same.

Once again another tiny chirp of a sound broke the quiet. Tommy spun in a circle, only to end on the nearest mine entrance.

Leanne didn't hesitate to rush toward the location Tommy narrowed in on. "Willow? Jaybird?" She ducked under the sagging beam over the opening. "Are you here?"

Tommy tugged her back out into the sunshine. When she fought, he tightened his arms around her waist. "Easy. Look at that opening. We've got to be careful, who knows how much the structure inside has weakened. They may not be in here, even."

"Thomas." She spun on him. "Please."

"I know, I know." He held out his hand. "Give me a minute."

She rubbed her hands on her arms. The ten seconds she'd had her head in the mine shaft she'd gotten a chill. She knelt before the entrance. This time she didn't shout, and hoped the mine would carry her voice. "Jaybird? Willow? Are you in there?"

This time she was certain she heard a noise in response. Only the crunch of gravel signifying Tommy's return kept her in place. He knelt beside her with some semblance of a torch. "Wasn't much in the way of fuel around here, but I got what I could on it. We'll need some light."

"I know I heard something this time. I think they're in there." She rose. "So let's go."

"Yes, ma'am. Just like I said before, do as I say. If I say to go back, do so quickly and carefully. Hopefully they aren't far in, but if they are we could be on shaky ground fast."

"Fine. Fine. I'll listen. Let's go, please."

He shook his head in response to her impatience, but pulled a small box of matches out and lit the torch. "Willow? Jaybird? We're coming in. Don't be scared."

The flickering flames of the makeshift torch gave off a little heat but did little to warm the pit of concern in her belly. She kept one hand on Tommy's back so he wouldn't be concerned about where she was.

Much as she wanted to look ahead, her full focus went on her feet and where they were going to find purchase on the uneven ground. They both heard a familiar clicking and roze. Someone had cocked a gun.

Leanne lifted her gaze to find the source. The light flickered across some fallen beams, the signs of a cave-in clear ahead of them. After a few moments searching she saw the small, pale face peeking out from between two beams. She gasped. "Jaybird."

Tommy's arm flashed out to stop her progress. "Jaybird. We've got no one with us. No one's going to hurt you. Please put the gun down."

Once Tommy pointed it out, she could see the tip of the gun pointing out from a break in the boards below the boys head. Leanne knelt down to Jaybird's eye level. "Jaybird. Where is your sister? Is she all right?"

Tears welled in his eyes, each gleaming in the torch light. He shook his head.

"Can I come see?" At Tommy's grunt, she sighed. "Can we please come see? We might be able to help. Or at least get you out of the cold. It's not safe here."

In his panic, the boy jabbered in the unfamiliar language for several minutes.

"Jaybird," Leanne soothed. She rose and crept toward the boy, well aware Tommy and his torch were hot on her heels.

Somehow Tommy got ahead of her and took the weapon from the distraught child. He cursed under his breath. "Leanne get over there. Carefully."

She squeezed around him in the tight space. Curled against her brother, Shivering Willow was pale, her lips near blue. Shallow breaths made her jump gently. The dirty clothes she'd been given were torn, the shirt hanging on by a bare thread.

Leanne had no idea how she held her tears at bay as she knelt next to the girl. She ignored the clicks of Tommy disarming the gun to get down near Shivering Willow's level. One gentle touch to the girls cheek sent her into a flail of panic. A sharp wheeze echoed through the small space.

"Easy. It's me, Willow. You're going to be okay. Jaybird." Leanne set her hand on Jaybird's to ease his chattering. "I don't speak Ute, remember? Now we need to help your sister. Did you bring her medicine?"

He held the pouch toward her. "No work."

"It's not working?" Leanne pulled the small pouch open to hold near Willow's mouth and nose. "Maybe she's been too scared. You both have."

"It's not safe in here," Tommy spoke low, his tone a touch higher pitched than normal. "Not structurally, and this chill could make then both sick. We have to see if she'll let me carry her."

Leanne nodded in agreement, even if she doubted it were possible just then. "Willow. We have to get you out where it's safer. Can you trust me?"

The girl's one visible eye focused on Leanne. A dark purple ring of exhaustion lingered in what should have been young, fresh skin. Her eye closed again, soft wheezes renting the silence.

"Please, Willow. Tommy has to carry you out of here. He won't hurt you. I promise. He would never hurt you. Please try not to panic, you'll make yourself sicker." Leanne brushed her fingers across Willow's forehead. "I'll help Jaybird, okay?"

The girl offered a weak nod.

Leanne sighed and rose best as she could. When Tommy offered the torch, she took it willingly and held out her free hand to Jaybird. The boy's cold fingers slipped into hers. She did her best to ignore the breathless yelp behind them a few moments later. When everything seemed to calm within a few minutes, she pushed forward.

They crept carefully out of the cave. Once in the sunshine, Leanne tossed aside the torch and kicked dirt on it to put out the flame. When she turned her attention fully on the children in the bright, unforgiving sunlight her heart broke.

"Oh. What happened to you two?"

* * * *

Tommy moved toward one of the abandoned tents. At least there he'd have a flat surface to set Willow down. After her initial panic, the girl had all but passed out. The bag of medicine her brother had managed to bring with them despite what appeared to be a broken arm dangled precariously in her slack fingers.

He laid Willow down on the rough hewn wood that had once made up the floor of the tent. Before he could say a word, Leanne was hiking her skirts. Layers of white petticoats crumpled to the boards. She handed him some, then set another layer over the girl on the boards.

Tears glimmered on her lashes, but she hadn't lost control. "We need to get them back to town. Daisy won't be here for another couple of days. Will she survive, Tommy?"

"She will if I have anything to say about it." Tommy turned his attention on the boy who stood watching them with a careful eye. With his left hand, he cradled his right arm against his chest. "We should make you a sling, Jaybird. It'll protect your arm."

Leanne frowned. "I'm fresh out of petticoats."

"There's some leftover clothing and muslin in a few of these tents. So long as they aren't too filthy, he should be fine." Tommy met her gaze, then nodded when she hesitated. "Right. If she wakes it oughtn't be me here."

A weak smile replaced her deep frown. "Sorry."

While he wandered through the debris looking for both fabric to fashion a sling, and anything they could use for a litter to carry the girl back. They didn't have long before they'd have to head back in order to not worry Reverend McGonagall. While he could carry the girl, that was less than ideal, all things considered.

When he returned, Willow's eyes were open, but her breathing was still abnormal. Short, wheezing gasps were all she could manage, and she still couldn't hold onto her bag of medicine. Bruises dotted the right side of her face, and the bruised impression of hands covered her upper arms.

When he set the old sheet he'd torn into a sling around Jaybirds arm, he noticed similar bruising on the boy's wrist. "We're going to have to get you both back."

"No." Jaybird shook his head firmly.

"Jacob and Lucy are dead. No one is going to hurt you. Leanne and I, we'll make sure of it." Tommy didn't have to seek out Leanne to know she agreed. He set a hand on Jaybird's shoulder. "We have to go back and get their bodies, and to get the reverend. You won't stay there any longer. Promise."

"White promise means nothing," Leanne whispered. "I told her what I'd do what I could to help her. I promised. Now this."

"You couldn't know. We thought visiting daily would be enough." Tommy focused on Jaybird. "You want to help me get a litter together to carry your sister? It'll be faster, and won't scare her so much if she woke to find me carrying her."

Jaybird frowned, but nodded.

"Is there water somewhere close?" Leanne turned toward them. "Both the children could probably use some, and I'd like to clean off some of this blood."

"I saw a well over there. Not sure the water is usable, but we'll check." Tommy guided the hesitant boy away from his sister. Together they worked to build a litter using scraps of different materials around the abandoned camp.

At the well he wasn't surprised to find it rank with some dead animal that had probably fallen into the wide hole in the boards.

Jaybird's nose wrinkled at the stench.

Tommy smiled. "Don't worry. I'm not going to make you drink that. We'll get water at the creek. We should get moving. Reverend McGonagall will get worried if we aren't back soon." Luckily on the return route they wouldn't have to move as slow as they had coming this way. With the children in hand, there was no further need to look for a trail.

Their pace would be dictated only by the fact they carried the young lady in the litter. If they got a good hold and a steady pace, they would be back in no time.

He carried the litter back to where Leanne sat with the girl. Jaybird ran on ahead. When Tommy set down the litter, Leanne rose. Her small hand on his chest was enough to push him back several feet away.

She took a shaky breath. "I don't think Jacob succeeded in violating her, I won't know for sure until she is awake, but there is little doubt he tried. Has Jaybird said anything about what happened?"

"He's barely said two words." Tommy pulled her into a gentle embrace. "Let's get them back to town. Unless the reverend knows of a place we can all lie in for the night, the children will come to our room and use the bed."

"Agreed. Let's get back before McGonagall starts to worry. How long have we been gone?"

"Nearly the two hours we said. Think you can move fast while carrying her?"

"I'll do whatever I need to." She brushed her hands on her muddy skirt as if that would help clean them off in any way. "Let's get moving."

After a little discussion, they each chose an end to carry from. With Jaybird's awkward help they loaded Shivering Willow on the makeshift litter. He checked on Leanne once more. The usually elegant woman was filthy, unkempt, and lines of concern added a maturity to her features normally absent.

If the time weren't so horrible he'd have said it was the most beautiful he'd ever seen her. He shook off the thoughts and counted so they would lift together.

The return walk was difficult and uncomfortable, but no one complained. Before they made it to where they needed to cross the creek, they heard the reverend calling. Tommy raised his voice to respond. "We're coming. We found the children."

The boy moved nervously closer to his sister, but made no sound.

Tommy took a deep breath. He'd made a promise and intended to keep it, but who knew what they'd face over the next few days. Nobody cared a lick about the kids before, but who knew what would happen when they learned who'd taken them in, and how they'd come to his and Leanne's care.

One thing was for sure, Daisy couldn't get there fast enough. Both children needed medical care. Much as he was loathed to admit it, he wondered if Leanne wasn't right about contacting Nick. He'd have to do that first thing the next morning when the telegraph office opened.

He'd thought he was doing right keeping the kids where they were from. Things weren't working out to well toward that end.

Perhaps a new environment would be a good thing. A place where they knew the people and knew where not to house the children.

Didn't it just figure Leanne would be right all along?

Chapter 12

Shivering Willow woke in a panic soon as they got her in the wagon. While Leanne and Jaybird calmed her down best as they could, Tommy pulled aside Reverend McGonagall. "We're keeping them with us at least until we can be sure Willow is going to pull through."

"Mr. Young," McGonagall sighed.

"I don't care that we're strangers, or what the town thinks Leanne is."

"Do not misunderstand. My protest isn't about anything but where you are boarding currently. It's not a good place for children, and the crowds can get rowdy." McGonagall shuffled his hand around in his hands.

"Do you know of anywhere else we can rent a room or two? I'll gladly take it, I'm sure Leanne would as well." Tommy smiled when the reverend's shoulders sagged. "The doctor should be here in a couple of days. I'll be wiring my brother in the morning. He's a lawyer, might be able to help us get the children situated somewhere better."

"You don't know anyone that might take the children? Being what they are, and all."

"I honestly don't know for certain without talking to them face to face." Tommy lifted his hat from his head to let in some cool air. "Once we get the girl well-taken care of and find out what happened at the farm, what would you say to me taking them with us?"

"Given what's happened here, whatever it was, it may be best." The reverend shook his head. "I don't like taking them from their home."

"This hasn't been their home for a long time, Reverend. The boy doesn't even remember. They've already been taken from their home and family thanks to the army. Best we can do for them now is find them somewhere they won't suffer more."

"Thomas." Leanne approached, one delicate hand wiped sweat from her forehead to leave a smudge of dirt behind. "We'd best be going. I don't know what we can do for her. She's looking worse. I'm afraid we might lose her."

"Reverend." Tommy turned to McGonagall. "Would you protest much if we had the telegraph office opened to send and receive a few telegrams? We have a couple of doctors in Dominion Falls. One might be on their way here, but the other might be able to tell me how best to help Shivering Willow."

"To save a life, the Lord will forgive." McGonagall nodded. "It's best we move fast and do what we can before any more lives are lost today."

Tommy rushed to load the deceased couple into the back of the wagon. After he'd covered them so Willow wouldn't see them should she wake again, he hopped into the front. This time the ride to town was brutally fast, but not even Leanne squeaked in protest. Her only response was to move into a different position so she could hold Willow on the narrow board that spanned the back of the wagon for seating.

Not one soul missed their loud arrival back in town. Even the whores lounging in the shade of the closed saloon drew close to see the excitement. Tommy pointed to Enid and another whore, "You and you. Bring us buckets of water, extra blankets and some hot water. There's an extra five dollars in it if you do it quick. Twenty more if you tell me there are medical supplies somewhere still in this damned town."

Enid's features lit up. "Doc's office is closed, been so for two years, but his old nurse squirreled all the supplies away so's no one would steal them. Think she thinks he's still comin' back or something. Bessie was in love with him."

Tommy noticed McGonagall open his mouth to protest the gossip, but cut him off. "Twenty dollars if you get her to bring a medical bag and as much medicine as the two of you can carry. I don't know what we'll need."

Enid nodded and rushed down the street, calling for Bessie as she went.

Tommy gently took Willow from Leanne. When he turned back the other whore was still staring at him, and two others behind her. "You're all going to pass on five dollars each? Move. Quickly."

He ignored the cries of townspeople that stuck their curious noses under the tarp in the back seat. Leanne didn't get off so lucky as she had to find her way out of the wagon with Jaybird while the crowd gathered round.

If he could help, he would, but the barely breathing form in his arms had to take priority. Inside the saloon, Loren stood by the window staring out at the crowd. "Loren."

The man cast a suspicious glare his direction.

"Help get those two out of the wagon, would you? I don't want a mob attacking them. The boy is injured too."

"What do I care?" He sniffed and turned away from the window.

"I've got more money than your banker friend, and can easily shut his bank down with a few well place telegraphs. Your biggest source of income gone. Poof."

Loren narrowed his eyes. "You're why he ain't here."

"You bet I am. Now go help or he won't be back. We'll discuss the twins once we get the kids settled."

"They ain't for sale."

"Tell it to someone who cares." Tommy stormed up the steps to the room he and Leanne had been sharing. He set Willow down with care to not wake her. At this point he wasn't sure she could be woken, but one more panic attack, and he wasn't sure she'd be breathing at all.

As it stood, her lips were blue, her color pale.

Noise clamored up the stairs, and two of the whores lugged in buckets of water. Neither of them had muslin or hot water, but they both held out their hands. He dug in his pocket and handed them each a five dollar bill.

Leanne burst into the room with Jaybird, panic drawing her eyes wide. "They're accusing the children of murder. It's a horrible mess."

"I don't care. The children will stay here and that's that. First problem is getting Shivering Willow well cared for." He glanced at the whores that were admiring the bills in their hands. "Where's the rest of what I asked for?"

"Ain't sure if Enid'll manage it, but Annie's getting your hot water and such. Hold your horses. Water's got to boil like you asked." She grinned broader and fanned herself with the money she held. "Anything else ya need? Happy to take care of you."

"He's well taken care of." Leanne stepped between him and the two whores. "Take your eager selves on out of here. Go on. Get!"

The girls obeyed without question. Tommy grinned. "I guess they know a madam's tone when they hear it."

"They always do." Leanne propped on the edge of the bed. "You have to go send your telegrams. There's no way around it."

"I know. Let me tell you what to do with the stuff. I'll make sure Loren locks up tight no matter what so you'll be safe enough. Only let Enid in the room, and the nurse if she comes, though I doubt she will."

Leanne nodded. "We'll survive, and maybe you can calm the crowd. They certainly wouldn't listen to me."

"I'll do what I can."

* * * *

Leanne left Jaybird on the bed with his sister to comfort her. His hushed words didn't cause a flicker of an eyelash in the unconscious girl on the bed. With a shudder at the grim sight, Leanne popped apart the buttons of her bodice.

She went behind the curtain long enough to slip into a much simpler cotton dress. Once again Jane's over-packing came to her rescue for she would have otherwise had no use for such an outfit, but Jane had insisted as it took up little room.

When Leanne stepped out from the room divider, Jaybird himself was half-dozing. His injured arm tucked between the two, his good hand on his sister's shoulder. A knock at the door caused his eyelids to flicker open.

She offered him what she could only hope was an encouraging smile. At the door she hesitated. Given the scene she'd left outside, her nerves were on edge. "Who is it?"

"Enid. I brung as much of the doctor's stuff I could carry." Enid's arms were so full, it was a wonder nothing toppled to the floor.

Leanne pulled the door all the way open to allow her in. Soon as the tail of the blanket Enid dragged behind her crossed the threshold, Leanne shut the door again. "The nurse wouldn't come?"

"You kiddin'? Bessie Lorant wouldn't stoop to coming within fifty feet of no saloon." Enid snorted and laid everything out across the table. "She gave me everything though, once I told her it was a kid. I just didn't tell her which one."

"Thank you." Leanne looked through the bag, unsure what half of the items were. When she saw the word 'chloroform' she paused. "Here. Tommy said to use a couple drops of this. It's supposed to help."

Enid watched in silence as she went to the dresser. "Anything else I can do?"

"No one ever brought us hot water. Tommy said the steam might help." Leanne pulled a handkerchief from the top drawer. She put a couple of small drops of chloroform on the cloth square and crossed back to the bed. "Hopefully Charlie tells him what to do. My medical knowledge is limited to small injuries. And I hate blood."

"They gonna be okay?"

"He will be, physically. I'm not so sure about her. We just have to watch and do our best to help her." Of course, the trauma of what they'd been through was a whole other story.

"Well, I'm not much for praying these days, but I'm pulling for 'em." Enid moved to the door. "I'll get that water for ya. Be back soon."

"Thank you, Enid." Leanne got up long enough to lock the door before she returned to table and grabbed a chair to put bedside. She took a seat and held the kerchief about an inch from Willow's face as Tommy had instructed.

After a few minutes her breathing appeared to ease a little. Leanne set the kerchief on the table and dropped a cup over it. Another knock on the door didn't even wake the boy from his slumber. She wondered if he'd slept at all the night before.

She rose and crossed to the door. "Who is it?"

"It's me." Tommy's tone was quiet as hers.

"Thank goodness." She pulled the door open. "Enid's getting hot water the other girl didn't bring. The chloroform seemed to help a little, but she still isn't well."

"Good. Charlie sent me a long list of suggestions. I'll have to go through all of the items Enid brought to see what I can do. I know there's several things, including the herbs from her medicine bag that we can add to the steam to help. We'll have to get her sitting to do it proper, though." Tommy squeezed her shoulder. "I imagine we'll be getting another telegram from Jane soon too, once she hears."

"What about the crowd? Were you able to talk them down at all?" She set her hand on his, grateful he kept it there for several minutes. The simple comfort did wonders for her frayed nerves and exhausted body. "They both need baths, but I loathe taking them from this room under these conditions."

"They're as settled as they're going to get." After one more squeeze, he released his hold on her shoulder. He sat beside her to look through the medicine and supplies on the table. "Especially since we aren't sure what happened out there."

"They can't think the children—"

"They can, and do. For all we know they may even be partly right, depending on the situation. I've got Jacob and Lucy on ice until we know more, and Daisy gets here."

"Daisy?" Leanne frowned. "What can she do about two dead souls?"

"Not much with their souls, but she can do an autopsy. Lucy's reason for death is pretty clear, she got shot twice. Jacob, not so much. He's been shot in the side, but nothing that looks too fatal, and he was hit in the head, too. Not sure what, exactly, killed him. Knowing that might help us figure out who did it."

"I see." Truthfully, she didn't entirely see. Exhaustion was making her brain fuzzy enough without help from Tommy's sharp logic and years of law experience.

"Do you really?" He stopped his search to meet her gaze. A hint of a smile tugged the corner of his mouth until his moustache twitched.

She pursed her lips. "Don't make fun of me."

"I'm not."

"You are."

"Maybe a little. I'm really just teasing you because you are tired."

She nodded. "I very much am. I'm not ready to sleep yet, though. There's too much to do. Tell me what I can do to help."

"When Enid arrives with the hot water, get it in the bowl. Put in some of her medicine bag and we'll get her sitting over it." Tommy patted her hand. "We'll get her taken care of. Promise."

"Shivering Willow said white promises mean nothing."

"How about a Pink's promise?"

Chapter 13

The night had passed torturously slow. Leanne and Tommy traded off watching over the children. In the morning Leanne insisted on getting them food, and more hot water for Shivering Willow's treatments.

They didn't expect Daisy until the following day, and though Willow showed signs of improvement, anything close to healthy lingered far away. Jaybird had to get some morphine to help the pain in his arm. Tommy had, once the child slept, set the arm properly and placed a splint. The event had been painful and traumatic for the boy, and Leanne as well.

Tommy gave her a light warning to keep an eye peeled for trouble outside. Though he had calmed the situation for the time being, who knew what the light of day would bring. Once she'd revealed the Derringer she kept on her person, he'd let her go without another word.

At the top of the stairs she ran into Enid, surprised to see a stack of muslin in her arms. "Good morning, Enid."

"Morning. Thought I'd bring some fresh muslin. Thought ya might need it."

"That's very thoughtful. Thank you." Leanne smiled and moved to pass her. Two steps down, she paused. "Would you be able to get more hot water to Tommy for me? I'm going to go get some food for us, and hopefully some broth to feed to Willow."

"Sure. Monday's our slow day anyhow. Ain't got nothing else to do."

"Thank you." Leanne continued on her way, happy to check one task off her list. On her way out the door, she remained keenly aware of the dark look Loren kept focused on her. She ignored him, too focused on her task to care much.

She ran her errands with little trouble, but some whispers and some attitude from the owner of the small restaurant in town. After a pass by the mercantile for fruit, cheese, and some crackers with honey for a treat, she returned to the saloon.

Soon as she entered, Loren fixed her with another dark stare. Sick of the silent war he seemed to enjoy besetting her with she approached. She set the heavy basket on the bar and met him stare for stare.

Leanne leaned on the bar, refusing to balk at his sneer. "What?"

"They ain't yours any more than them kids."

"First, I never claimed they were, or would one day be my kids. I am human and care, more than can be said for most of the people in this town. As for the twins, which I assume you meant, we'll see about that."

"You'll see. I ain't selling their contract."

"And that would be a grave mistake. See, I have money to give you, a really good amount, more than they're worth in their current conditions." Leanne settled herself on the chair. "Whiskey, please."

Loren didn't move until she tossed two quarters on the counter. He poured slow. "I get plenty for 'em."

"Sure you do. You get, what, fifty dollars a week from your so-called generous benefactor? Meanwhile he causes injuries as he takes his pleasures. Am I right?"

Rather than answer, Loren merely grunted and wiped down the counter.

"That money barely covers your opium indulgence every week, I'd bet. Maybe a little extra pocket change. For those minor injuries you probably have to pay Miss Lorant a pretty penny to lay a finger on your whores to help them."

"I do well enough without." Loren lifted his chin.

"And when the injuries become more severe? They always do. When you give a man like that an inch, he'll take a mile every time. Especially now that by denying me you're essentially giving him ownership of them. You hold their contract, but he holds the cards."

Loren stopped wiping the counter to focus on her.

"When things go too far there's no doctor here, and the nurse won't help, and your prized whores will get damaged. They'll lose their draw for even your poorest patron. Or, God forbid, he could kill one. Then it'll all be over for you."

He lifted his chin and glared down his nose at her.

"Of course, there's also the fact that they wanted to leave so bad they used deception to get me here. They want out, and they are smart, clearly. One way or another those girls are leaving. They'll take off and face death and jail rather than stay here any longer. I've seen girls like this before, and believe me, when they get their minds set, they do it."

"They'd never make it out of town."

"Believe what you want, but if they tricked you once, they can do it again. There's two of them ready to run.

Wouldn't you rather profit from their desires instead of lose all that income without any recourse?"

He shook his head. "Wouldn't want that."

"Exactly. Easiest way I see is you could take what I'm offering and be well taken care of for some time if you're careful with it. You could get several whores for what I'm offering, or get yourself out of this dead town. Whatever you want."

He lowered his gaze and resumed wiping the counter.

"It's your choice, Loren. I want to meet the girls before I make my offer, but trust me on this. If I like what I see, you won't be disappointed."

She downed her whiskey before he could answer. With one brief nod to him, she took the basket and made her way upstairs. She found Enid and Tommy at the top of the steps. Enid's eyes were wide, but Tommy bore a grin that warmed her to her belly.

"Nice job. Knew you had it in you." He held out his hand for the basket. "They're both asleep, I just came out to see if you were back. Got treated to a show."

"Hush, you." She handed off the basket, but warmth filled her cheeks at her praise. "You act as though I haven't been a woman of business for over ten years now."

"Never seen you in action to that extent, is all." He winked. Before he stepped away he nudged his head Enid's direction. "See you inside."

Leanne furrowed her brow in confusion as he disappeared.

Enid shook her head. "Ain't ever seen a woman talk to him that way."

"Well, more women should." Leanne chuckled. "Thank you for all your help, Enid."

"No need."

"Enid." An idea struck her before she could get too far. Maybe the idea was Tommy's and why he'd nodded to Enid, but she'd claim it for her own. "Have you thought at all about joining us in Dominion Falls?"

"What? Oh, no. I only got two years left here. Got plans for after. Ain't gonna get stuck nowhere else."

"I admire that, but you misunderstood." Leanne stepped closer and spoke low. "More pay, better clientele, nicer clothes, and no time added on your current contract. I wouldn't keep you a minute over whatever time you have left."

"I…"

"Just think about it." Leanne set a hand on Enid's shoulder. "You've been a great help these past couple of days, and Tommy thinks you're of good stock, so that means something. If you can get better, you should always think about it."

Enid blinked a few times. "Ain't no one nice as you two."

"Not entirely true. That's something you have to learn for yourself. I hope we can help you do that."

"I, um…" Enid jumped when Loren barked her name. "Better get goin'."

"I suppose so. My offer stands. We'll be here another few days at least. Plenty of time for you to think."

Enid's cheeks flushed, but she darted down the stairs.

Leanne went back to the room, not surprised to find the door open. Tommy leaned on the wall just inside. She raised her brows. "Is that what you intended to happen?"

"Just about."

"You're a sneaky bastard sometimes. Next time just tell me what you're thinking."

He tucked his hand under her elbow and pulled her close. "Do I always have to tell you? Or can I show you sometimes, too?"

"Depends on what the situation calls for, I suppose."

He cut her off with a kiss that made her tingle down to her toes.

* * * *

When Leanne's warm lips softened under his and her body leaned into his, Tommy could hardly remember the children in the room behind them. Great effort went into ending the kiss, and by the look of her heavy lids and lopsided smile, Leanne had briefly forgotten the children as well.

He smiled in response. "Sorry, couldn't resist."

"Never resist." Her voice was husky, her breath short. "Please, not ever again."

"Wish I didn't have to, but the children are still here."

"Oh, oh, right." Her lashes fluttered as she came to her senses. "Goodness. How could I have forgotten?"

"A good kiss'll do that to a person."

"And here I thought Jane was full of nonsense when she claimed such things." A pleasant pink flush filled her cheeks as she scuttled into the room around him. "I suppose I should know better than to doubt a soul with such experience."

"Please don't discuss my sister's level of experience."

"You lived in the room next door to her for over a year." Her soft laughter didn't stir the two children on the bed.

"Precisely why I don't care to discuss it." He peeked in the basket she'd brought along with her. "You got some treats."

"I thought some crackers and honey would be a tasty snack. I also snuck a few pieces of candy for Jaybird. I'm not sure that he's ever had proper candy, I thought it would be a treat." She drew a small covered pot out of the basket. The whole thing remained wrapped tight in towels. "Some broth for Willow."

"You did good." He set his hands on her shoulders, surprised to find how much she sagged as the tension left. "You're no incapable woman. Why are you so surprised?"

"I've dealt with many things in my life. My bastard father trying to kill my sister. My sister herself. My mom dying. Being a whore that wasn't a whore. Men, so many men." She glanced toward the bed. "But much as I cared for my sister, there was always someone there taking the lead. I've never dealt with something like this. These small, scared children. No matter whether Willow is a young lady, she's been taken from her family, and that makes her small and scared as much as it does her brother."

"Breathe." He turned her toward him. Far as he could tell she hadn't taken one breath in her rambling. "You needn't be so nervous. Your instincts are leading you well."

"Sorry." She took a deep breath and released it through pursed lips. 'It's just a lot to happen. Your crazy family may be used to dealing with such chaos, but I'm not. I'm not Jane."

"You definitely aren't." He pulled out a chair, glad she sat immediately. "Let's get some food in you. I think lack of food is wearing you down."

"Right. Of course. Sorry." A smile crossed her features as she drew her gaze away from the bed again. "Let's eat, then. They didn't have much selection. There's a little meatloaf and fried potatoes. I doubt they'll measure up to Cora's, but they'll pass muster hungry as we are, I suspect."

"And we can follow up with one of those apples. They look good, at least." Tommy unloaded their food from the basket. He set aside the plate she'd gotten for Jaybird in case the boy woke.

Before he sat, he went to check on Willow one more time. Thankfully she was breathing smoother now, if not deep enough to return normal color to her lips.

When he sat back down, he met Leanne's questioning gaze. "She is breathing steadier. We've got that much going for her."

"It's so painful for her when we get her up for the steam. I'm almost loathed to do it. Jaybird needs to eat, though. It'll be good to get him up and have him eat at the same time."

"That's why we're eating first. We'll need the fortification to put her through that again." He patted her hand before he dove into his food.

Leanne ate more delicately, rather she picked at her food.

"Eat."

"Fine." After she'd eaten a few full bites she offered him a glare. "Better?"

"Yup."

Now that she'd eaten a few bites, Leanne seemed to notice she was hungry and dove in with more enthusiasm. It wasn't until her meatloaf was nearly gone that she slowed. A few bites later, she glanced at him sideways. "Tell me about your wife."

The potatoes congealed in his mouth until Tommy had to force himself to swallow. Over the past couple of years they'd talked about a great many things. His ex-wife had never once been a topic of conversation. He cleared his throat, and promptly choked on the lump of potato still stuck in his throat.

By the time he'd managed to regain composure, she was staring at her near-empty plate. "Sorry. I shouldn't have."

"No. Not that." Tommy cleared his throat and took a long sip of water. "You just surprised me. That's all."

"You never talk about it. I've been told the subject is not to be broached, and all you ever said was you were a Pink and that's how it ended." She pushed around the remaining potatoes with her knife. "But you never talk about her."

"Didn't know you wanted to know." He adjusted the napkin on his lap to buy time.

"Well, I was…it wasn't…things now are…oh, devil."

A smile crept up despite the serious conversation. He realized why the topic had come up now. "You mean this is more than playful now."

"So Jane was right. We've agreed to not tell her, but yes." She cleared her throat. After she'd set her knife down, she leveled her gaze on him. A nervous twitch settled in the corner of her delicate lips, but otherwise she remained focused. "I'd like to know, but you don't have to tell me. I'd like to know more about you."

"Well, all right then." He wiped his mouth with his napkin. "Nora was from a good family, one of the wealthiest in town. Her dad was a lawyer, and she was well educated. Quiet, but funny. That woman could make anyone laugh."

Leanne smiled, and his guilt over talking about his ex-wife alleviated somewhat. "You loved her, clearly."

"I did. Ma raised us to think about station, but not rely on it." Tommy pushed his plate forward to lean his forearms on the table. "When I signed up for the Pinkerton's she objected. I talked her into it. She could make people laugh, I'm good at convincing people to do what they don't want to do."

"I think everyone knows that."

"She turned out to be right. The job was everything I said it would be, and everything she said it would be. I had to leave all the time. She wanted to raise a family, but didn't want to when I could go anywhere in the country, or the frontier, on assignment. I could have requested all my tasks be closer to home, I know I should have but…"

"You didn't want to stay put. Sometimes you still don't." Her words sent a shock through him. A soft hand on his pulled his gaze to hers. "I see the way you watch the train leave."

"Sometimes the itch hits again. I'm plenty happy in Dominion Falls, but once in a while the urge strikes. In my youth, it struck all the time." He took a deep breath. "Then I got the plum assignment, to guard President Lincoln."

"She didn't like it?"

"You know how I told you she was quiet? Well, when I told her she wasn't quiet any longer. She railed at me for hours, and none of my logical counters worked. I could only see the honor in the role, she could only see the danger." His heart twisted as he remembered the tears in her eyes when it came down to an ultimatum. "She said it was her or the President."

"Oh."

"You know us stubborn Young's. I thought she was just upset and would calm down, that she'd see what I was doing. So I told her to calm down and we'd talk on my first trip home." He took a deep breath. "I made it to my hotel to find the divorce papers. I thought long and hard on signing or going home."

Her hand squeezed his.

"I knew my wanderlust wasn't done. The war was brewing and the President was going to need a lot of protection. I thought she'd be happier if she was free to obtain what she wanted. Young's are good at logic, even when it hurts like hell."

"I'm so sorry."

He tried to force up a happier smile. "Turns out my logic was sound. She remarried a few years later. Has a litter of kids to rival Jane's. We used to send letters. When I settled in Dominion Falls, they dropped off. I think it bothered her that I stopped moving around."

She took a shaky breath. "My goodness. I appreciate knowing, but I'm sorry I brought up such pain for you."

"It's more a dull ache to talk about now. That was years ago. She's not the only one that's moved on with her life and set a new future."

The blush darkened her cheeks again. "Is that so?"

"My reverse Madam Bovary, do you have to ask?"

"I might."

"Well—"

Leanne jumped when Jaybird stirred enough to release a yelp. She turned in her chair. "Well, Jaybird. Good afternoon. Are you hungry?"

Tommy squeezed her hand and rose. "We've got some food here for you. Why don't you eat up, and we'll get your sister another treatment."

Leanne rose, but he stopped her from moving to the bed yet. She leaned back against him at his gentle tug.

He spoke low in her ear. "We aren't done talking."

"Glad to hear it."

Chapter 14

Tommy made certain Leanne and the children were well settled before he left the room. Though the quiet that descended once both children were placed in bed would have been the perfect opportunity to continue his talk with Leanne, he had to get to the telegraph office.

Between the kiss, and the revelation of his marriages demise, somehow he felt closer to Leanne than ever. The subtle way she touched him more often, and the lingering gaze she'd laid on him for the previous two hours gave him hope she felt the same.

Jane would be impossible to deal with when she found out, but he didn't see how they'd manage to hide it. At least for now their telegrams were long enough, and she wasn't present to tease him for it. So for the next several days he would be able to enjoy the change in relative quiet. He didn't suspect Daisy would be nearly as relentless as his sister.

The whole way to the telegraph office Tommy took notice of the cold, suspicious looks he received. Those were easy to ignore. The three men inside the office that all turned on him weren't so easy to ignore.

Still, Tommy wasn't one to pick a fight, even if he wouldn't turn away from one. "Mr. Sullivan. Have I got any wires?"

"Too many. Who's got this kind of time or money?" Sullivan turned and slapped down a small pile of telegraphs. "That'll be two bits just for the receiving."

Tommy tossed the money on the counter. He didn't bother to tell the man that Jane was best friends with the wife of Loren, Dominion Falls telegraph operator. Or that Jane had taken to learning how to send and receive telegrams on her own, which meant she could send them at a lower cost as well. It wasn't any of their business anyhow.

Jane had sent a multitude of questions about the children, which had increased after the events of the day before. It was a message about halfway through that gave Tommy pause. "Damn that woman," he muttered under his breath. She'd taken it upon herself to send Nick before he'd dared or cared to ask. Once again as 'company' for Daisy.

At least this time he knew Jane meant it as just that, company. Daisy had managed to get herself in a relationship with one of Tommy's other brothers, Mike. Jane had likely sent Nick for the dual purpose of protection for Daisy, and legal knowledge for the children.

Tommy took up a pad and pencil. One by one he answered Jane's questions on the children, both their white and Indian parents, and their current state of health. He addressed her sending of Nick with a mixture of gratitude and resentment.

On the very last wire, her words teased him even in black and white. *How is Leanne? Or do you even know yet? Nick will be there soon. You should move along, or move along.*

He chose not to answer the final question. Jane had an exacting memory and would know without a doubt he'd answered every single line except that final telegram. With a memory similar to his sisters, he calculated the amount of wires, and words, in his mind and retrieved enough money from his wallet to send them all.

Sullivan pulled the notes and money toward him. "It's pointless, ya know."

"He's right. Them kids ain't going nowhere. We already sent for the marshal. They're savages, like they were raised." The largest of the men leaned on the counter beside Tommy. "We'll take care of them."

"Mr. Warren." Tommy turned to face the man. He allowed a grin filled with venom to form as the man did a double take by Tommy's use of his name. "That's right, I know who you are. We met a long time ago, played cards together. You once used to force the teacher in town into bed, didn't you?"

"I…never." Warren took a few steps back.

"Clara Young. You remember her, most people that knew her do. You were superintendent back then. Threatened her job because of her—loose behavior—and took advantage of it." Tommy stared the man down. "She thought I didn't know, but you had a big mouth when you had enough rotgut in you."

"You don't know nothing."

"I know plenty. Including the fact that the Marshal, should he come, will wait for facts instead of jumping to conclusions. When the children can talk, and when the doctor arrives for their exams, and the autopsies of the bodies, we'll talk about what happens to the children."

Warren seemed to gather his senses after Tommy's mention of the past. "Jake and Lucy are dead, and the kid had Jake's gun on him. That's evidence enough."

"Of a scared child trying to protect his dying sister? Yes, I suppose it is. However, with his arm broken, and the size of the weapon, he could hardly lift it, much less fire. But believe what you will." Tommy turned to Sullivan. "I'll be right outside awaiting the reply. I have no doubt Miss Spencer is sitting in wait for those and will be right back with word."

He turned his back on the men. Though tense and prepared for an attack, he made it outside without any scuffle. A few minutes later the group left the office together, an almost argument between them. Hopefully that meant Tommy's suggestion of Warren's character was enough to weaken that bond.

Almost ten minutes later Sullivan called him back inside. This time there were but two telegrams waiting on him. The first simply commented on his avoidance of the topic of his relationship with Leanne. The other, far more succinct note kept his attention.

Bring them home soon as you can. We will find a place for them. Somewhere.

* * * *

Leanne covered her smile when Jaybird dug into his meal with relish. Since they'd returned to the room they'd all picked at their food, Jaybird especially. To see him regain some appetite delighted her to no end.

Unfortunately the boy still didn't talk much at all. It would help their situation if he would just tell the what had happened at that farm. Now and then he seemed poised to speak, but then he'd stop himself and resume his near-mute status.

She ran her fingers along his scalp, frowning slightly. "Would you let me brush out these knots, Jaybird? I doubt they're very comfortable." She toyed with the shorn ends of hair. When the children had been dragged into town she'd not noticed how his hair was hacked away.

The ends were in odd chunks. Even with his hair as tangled as the past few days had made it, she could see patches of hair that were clearly different lengths.

"Jaybird? Did the soldiers chop your hair?"

"With knife." He kept eating through his two-word speech.

"I see. Maybe we can get you another bath and I can cut it a little straighter."

He fairly growled. One hand shot to his head.

"All right. I only wanted to straighten it. I know it must have been frightening to have them hack it off that way. We'll leave it be for now." A small rustle from the bed drew both their attention. Leanne rose on the off-chance Shivering Willow might wake.

Over the course of the second night her breathing had finally eased. Leanne couldn't say it was a normal breath, but it was a fair sight better than it had been.

She approached the bed slow, careful not to scare the girl should she wake. Right as she set a hand on Willow's forehead, the girls eyes flew open. Leanne hushed Willow at the first gasp. "Easy, Shivering Willow. You're safe. Jaybird is here and you're safe."

Jaybird scrambled over Willow's legs fast as his broken arm would let him and curled at his sister's side. He spoke again in Ute, in low tones.

Leanne sank into the chair beside the bed. "You had us frightened, Willow. We have a doctor coming on the stage today that may be able to help you more." She set a hand on Willow's shoulder.

Willow's eyes fluttered shut when Jaybird spoke again. After a few minutes she turned to face Leanne, her eyes wide.

"No one will hurt you again, Willow. We'll see to it. I don't know what happened out there, but I know I won't let it happen again." Leanne took a shaky breath. "I know a white promise means nothing to you, but I promise. We'll take you somewhere you can be safe."

Shivering Willow's voice was but a whisper, but carried acres of panic in the language of the people that had raised them. A shudder carried through her and she took a wheezing breath.

"Shh. Don't panic, please. You just started to breathe somewhat well. Try to relax. Jacob and Lucy are gone. You're with Tommy and I for now. Soon as we get this all cleared up, we'll take you somewhere you won't have to be afraid like you were."

"Ma, Pa." Shivering Willow's eyes drifted closed.

"We saw them. They say it would not be safe for you on the reservation. They only want you safe." Leanne sighed when Willow's head drooped. She met Jaybird's gaze and offered the best smile she could muster. "She woke. That's a good sign. If she wakes again in a few minutes we'll try and get her some real food. How about that?"

Jaybird nodded.

"Good." Leanne rose at the quick pulse of knocks against the door that signified Tommy's return. She smiled as she pulled open the door. "Tommy. She woke for a few minutes."

"That's a good sign." He hauled in the refilled basket. "I brought us more food this time. Stage should arrive in a few hours, I want to be prepared to lay in for another night. I expect that Marshal will be here no later than tomorrow. We'll have to deal with that."

"So we are done talking for the time being." Leanne closed the door behind him. "At the very least any hope of peace and quiet is ruined."

"We still have a couple hours until the stage." Tommy leaned over to check on the children. Seemingly satisfied, he dropped into the chair beside her. "If you want, at least."

"Of course I do. Does this mean it's my turn to bare some truths?"

"Thought I knew everything already."

"You are many things, but stupid is not among them. Do you think a woman would reveal all to a man who holds himself back?" She peeked into the basket, wondering at how he'd carried the basket so laden with goods.

"I suppose not. What don't I know?"

"You know the basic facts. Of my relation to Cole, that my mother died, and he took me in under a pseudo-contract. You know little of what happened in truth."

"You have a point. In the same context as you knew I had a wife, but not what happened between us." He leaned forward. "So what shall we discuss?"

"What about the first time I met Cole?"

"That'll work."

"I was nearly eight. Ma was pregnant with Alma. One day after Pa visited, I saw Cole. I don't know what he was doing, exactly." A knock on the door interrupted her, and she rose. "Give me a minute."

"Just one," he teased.

She opened the door, surprised to find Enid on the other side. "Enid? Is everything all right?"

"Loren. He says you can meet the girls."

"Oh, wonderful." Leanne brightened. "Took him long enough. I'll be down shortly."

"No. He said now or never. He's in a right mood. I don't wanna cross him." Enid twisted her hands together.

Leanne glanced over her shoulder at Tommy. "Did you do something?"

"Not today. Promise. I saw you had it handled and haven't said a thing." Tommy held up his hands in defense.

"All right." She set a hand on Enid's twisted ones. "Why don't you have a sit with Tommy and relax, you look a mess."

"You shoulda never said nothing to me." Enid shook her head. "I was doing all right."

Leanne chuckled as she ushered her into the room. "Sit. Tommy, please see that she calms down before she heads back downstairs. And I guess we'll continue the story soon as we can. I really should go take care of this. It is what I came here for."

He nodded. "I know. But I expect my story."

"Maybe we'll make it a bedtime story."

"I sure would like that."

Chapter 15

Leanne did her best to keep her impatience to herself. Loren made a great show of searching for the proper key to the room where he'd ensconced the twins upon her arrival. She refused to give him the pleasure of knowing how annoyed she was by the whole needless push for dominance.

Instead she smiled and chuckled at his false apologies. Once he'd final managed to get the door open, she counted to three in her head before following to keep her calm air.

The room he'd locked them in stood smaller than Jane's closet, lined with shelves and one small cot of a bed. The window had boards nailed in crosswise, which left Leanne wondering how they'd made their grand escape attempt a few days before.

Their hands locked together, the girls stood at the same time upon seeing Leanne. Neither of them spoke, though the one on the left appeared to be under a great effort to keep silent. Loren gestured to them. "See. That's them. They ain't much."

Leanne allowed a half-smile. She straightened until she stood tall as possible. "I believe that is my determination to make. I'd like a few minutes with them. We'll discuss the matter after. Oh, and also, one of the doctor's will be here today to examine the children. I'd like them examined as well."

"What for?"

"You clearly think little about proper care or treatment of your whores. Who knows what mess the men you let near them would impart. I'd like to make sure I'm not purchasing whores that are likely to lose their minds to syphilis." She smirked. "It's just good business. I'm sure you understand."

He narrowed his eyes, but nodded. Rather than reply, he spit into the chamber pot and left the room.

Leanne sighed and shook her head. "Men will never get it through their skulls that some women are quite capable of running a business." She turned to face the twins, then turned her attention to the window.

"Thank goodness you came! We're clean. How soon can you get us out of here? We really need to get out of here. If you don't take us, who knows what will happen. We're sorry we lied, we had no other choice." The girl on the left took a deep breath after spitting everything out in one breath.

Leanne examined the window. "How did you get out of here?"

"What? Didn't you hear me?"

"Of course I did. Flo, right? And that makes you Nellie." Leanne smiled when the quiet one nodded. The pair were rather lovely, would likely be more so after a good bath. Being trapped in a small room did no one any favors. "I was just curious. Tommy said he met you two trying to escape out this window."

"We pulled off the boards. Saturday is busy enough no one will hear anything anyhow." Flo shrugged. "At his request, we went ahead and came back in."

"And we weren't sure if he was actually with you. We figured it was safer to be in the room with the window sealed should he run to alert Loren." Nellie spoke quieter than her sister, but no less articulate. "We could say he was drunk and be done with it."

"If he believed you, you mean." Leanne studied them. "Risky move, either way. What if one of the patrons had come around and seen you?"

"Loren wouldn't beat us. He hasn't beat a whore yet." Flo lifted her chin.

"No. He leaves that to the customers, doesn't he?" Leanne stepped closer. "Well, should your exam with Daisy go well, we'll be heading to Dominion Falls in a few days' time."

"A few days!" Nellie covered her mouth after the outburst. "Miss DuBois…"

Leanne held up her hands. "You won't be locked in here much longer. Soon as you've had your exam you'll be allowed fresh air and some freedom. So long as you don't run, I won't send Tommy after you—and trust me, he's the sort that would catch you."

The girls eyed each other in silence.

"I'm not harsh or difficult. I don't let men beat my girls, not for any sort of money. You'll be well cared for, you'll have regular medical check-ups, and access to whatever you want to expand your knowledge. A whore that can talk of worldly matters fetches a high price, and with you two it would be double. I'm pleased you both already know how to read and write."

After Leanne finished, both of them turned a smile on her. Flo nodded. "We learned young. Ma raised us right, it was Pa that did us wrong."

Nellie's smile faltered and she nudged her sister.

"Right. Sorry." Flo cleared her throat. "We still want the same terms. Same percentage. Even though we lied to get you here, we will deliver."

"You're so desperate to be out of here, I don't think you would have much of a leg to stand on if I were a lesser person I could take full advantage." Leanne smiled. "Fortunately, you have me you're negotiating with and I like what I see. So long as your exams today go well, you'll be in the clear, without any alterations to our originally discussed contract."

Nellie breathed a small sigh of relief. "Thank you."

Leanne leaned closer. "You've got a good head on your shoulders, Nellie. I'm guessing you came up with the contract terms. You did well. I just ask you both to have patience. I'll be having Doctor Pearson visiting with the children first. They're in more of a medically necessary state than you, but we will be by in a few hours."

"Thanks again." Flo held out her hand. "It'll be good working with you."

"And you, so long as you don't lie to me again we'll get along just fine." Leanne left the room without another word. So long as time allowed, she'd be nicer next time. It was better to let them stew. If they tried to run again, she'd know if it was worth her dime. If they stuck with it and did as told, she could make them work well in her house.

They'd spent a few years bucking the rules they were forced under. Only their fear had led them to Leanne. She didn't want to need fear to keep them around.

All she had left to wonder about was whether Enid would join them. Leanne knew the woman was intrigued by the offer. With any luck Tommy had managed some influence in the decision. Though the offer had been impulsive, Leanne could only imagine good coming from it.

Enid had shown signs of a stable mind, and had a goal in place. That had always meant a good, stable income in the right situation.

Leanne took a deep breath before she headed back down the hall. She ignored Loren passing her to lock the door back up. In a few hours Daisy would arrive, and perhaps along with her they'd gain some answers.

In the mean time they could only pray that Shivering Willow would wake enough to give some answers of her own. They needed to know what had happened, and Jaybird was not much of a talker.

Hopefully Willow continued to trust her, otherwise they could be left in the dark and without answers for the marshal.

* * * *

By the time Leanne returned, Tommy had both children out of bed. Enid had been good enough to take the linens out for him and bring them fresh. He managed to get Shivering Willow sipping down some soup.

His reward for all this effort came in the form of the bright smile Leanne wore as she approached. He even got a peck on the cheek.

She took a seat near him, and spoke low while Willow continued to eat. "I think they'll work out all right. We may have a few challenges smart as they are, but I'm sure we'll come to a good place. Has Enid said one way or another?"

"Not yet. I don't think she's yet figured out the offer is genuine. She's not one to believe in people being good for the sake of being good."

"I suppose that's true. They don't make a lot of people like us." She grinned and winked. "What time is the stage expected again?"

Tommy knew she remembered just fine, so the question and subject change were likely for the benefit of the children. "Two o'clock. We have a couple of hours before it arrives. Did I mention that Jane sent along Nick to keep Daisy company?"

A smarmy little hint of a smirk crossed her features. The damn woman knew she'd been right, but to her credit didn't say as much. "That was very thoughtful of Jane. I'm sure Daisy appreciates not having to travel alone, though she might have preferred the company of Mike."

"Mike's deputy, and with me gone can't leave. Plus, Nick has skills we're likely going to need with a few malcontents around here." Tommy didn't miss the way Willow's eating had slowed. The girl was listening intently. "Of course, knowing what happened could speed up the process of us all getting out of here. If either of you is ready to talk, that is."

Willow shook her head fast, and dove back into her soup.

Leanne rose to switch seats so she sat next to Willow. One delicate hand rested on the young lady's back, and the other settled on her wrist. "I understand it was scary, Willow. The last thing we want is for you to have to relive it, but two people are dead. We need to know what happened out there."

Tommy leaned forward. "If you want to wait until our friends get here so you only have to tell it once, that's all right. Please, think about it. We can get you both out of here faster if you tell. Once we get to Dominion Falls things will be different for you both."

"Ma. Pa." Shivering Willow wiped at her tears.

Leanne took a shaky breath. "They wanted you safe. They miss you terribly, but know it's not safe for you at the reservation."

Jaybird slipped under his sister's arm. She set down her spoon to hold him closer. "There is no safe."

"I know it seems that way. No one could blame you after what's happened to you." Leanne wiped away tears.

Tommy rubbed her back to ease her worries. All things considered, the children were doing remarkably well. "You have both been very strong. A good testament to your parents. They seem like good people. We promised them we would help you be safe. We can't do that if you are here."

"No choices," Willow whispered. Her weak breathing grew more rapid, her hand shaking slightly.

"I wish we had more for you. I wish it wasn't this way." Leanne handed Willow a handkerchief. "Take steady breaths. We'll get you more medicine soon. Easy."

Tommy rose as Leanne calmed the panicky girl. He heard her tell her to eat, they'd talk more soon. He glanced over his shoulder as she approached.

Leanne wrapped her hands around his bicep and leaned into him. Her head settled on his shoulder. When she spoke, the words were so quiet he could barely hear them. "What if we took them to see their parents just once? So they can properly say goodbye."

"I wish we could, but it's not possible. The army would never let them on that reservation."

"You know people." Her bright blue eyes focused on him. "Lots of people. You always say so. There has to be something we can do. If we don't do this right, there will be nothing that will ever make them feel right about any of it."

He didn't want to let her down, or the kids. There seemed little that could be possible in such a situation. He sighed softly. "I don't know, Leanne."

"There must be something. They'll never trust another soul but each other the way they're going. That's no way to live. Jane was proof enough of that when the only soul she trusted was Cole." She frowned. "Not to mention they'll never tell us what happened, not like this."

"Your pleas don't make it any more possible." He kissed the top of her head. "But I'll see what I can do. Don't take that as a promise or even a tiny ray of hope. There are some things that even I can't manage."

"Oh, I doubt that very much. You're a highly capable man."

"Flattery doesn't help either."

"Flattery always helps, you just are too stubborn to admit it."

He chuckled at her accuracy. "Fine, Madam DuBois. I forgot, no one is allowed to doubt your skill and knowledge. Forgive me for forgetting."

"You're forgiven."

"You've been very good with them, you know." He smiled when she lifted her head. "The children. You're a natural. All those years helping to raise Alma must have had quite the influence."

"You learn a certain level of patience." A flush pinked her cheeks.

"Ever thought about leaving the business and getting some of those for yourself?"

Her eyes grew wide and she glanced over her shoulder. "Honestly? No. It never crossed my mind. I'm not sure I ever want to. Have some of my own, that is."

Tommy was surprised by the revelation, only because he'd seen her with his nieces and nephews, not to mention how she'd been with Shivering Willow from day one. "Really? You really seem to like kids."

"Liking them, and having some I can't send to back to their mother are two different things. Why?" She snapped her gaze back on him. "I mean, what about you?"

"Never wanted them myself." He grinned at the sag of relief to her shoulders. "Being uncle suits me just fine."

"Well then. I guess…Well…"

"I agree."

The pink in her cheeks darkened further. "What was that about?"

"I think we just talked about the future."

"Our future?"

"I guess we'll find out."

Chapter 16

Tommy left Leanne with the children so he could greet the stagecoach. He had an almost embarrassing skip to his step after Leanne had graced him with soft kiss upon his departure. Acting like a love-struck youth was not something a man of his age needed to do, but damn if that woman didn't make him forget such things.

The way she'd cared for the children, despite having no intention of taking them in herself spoke volumes about her. Certainly he'd always known she had a good heart, but to see how intense she'd become with the children's path was a whole new level.

What she'd asked of him, to set up a meeting between the children and the Ute couple they considered parents, had initially seemed impossible. Whether it was the push of her affection, or the time he'd had to consider the option, it no longer seemed out of reach.

First he had to take care of his brother and Daisy. He'd already managed to wrench another room out of the tight grasp of Loren. The man was undeniably sour over the loss of the twins. Tommy could only imagine how grumpy he'd be when Leanne pushed for Enid as well.

The stagecoach rattled over a hill in the distance. Tommy's first priority would be to get Daisy to Shivering Willow, and then the bodies. He had a feeling Leanne's priority would stand at Willow, then the twins, and then the bodies. Possibly even have Enid thrown in the mix as well. He hoped Daisy was prepared to be in high demand for the first twenty-four hours.

Nick would mostly need to deal with the legal issues involved. Namely the town believing somehow that Jaybird had killed the couple. Tommy needed more answers, like the children's story and just how Jacob had passed. His gunshot wound hardly seemed fatal. Though he'd suffered a blow to the head, Tommy still wasn't sure that was the cause, either.

He lifted his head when the stagecoach drew to a stop a few feet away. Before the driver could set the steps, the door flew open. Daisy's head poked out. "Tommy."

"Dr. Pearson." He set his hands on her waist to help her down. Behind her Nick waited for the steps to be put in place. "I'm assuming you'd like to see the children?"

"Immediately. Nick has agreed to get my bags for me." She tipped her head toward Nick, her hand firm on Tommy's arm as he led her over. In her free hand she clutched her medical bag. "How is the girl doing now?"

"Better. This morning she woke and is eating on her own. She's still terrified and is prone to panicking, which doesn't help." He led her into the saloon where a call of protest greeted them.

"Wait just a daggum minute!" Loren circled the bar. "You said you were bringing the doctor. Where is he?"

"*He*," Daisy stepped right up to the saloon owner. The past few years had done wonders to help her regain confidence and shed her near-four years she'd worked as a whore. Of course, the recent epidemic where they'd suffered some great losses had left her sour most of the time. Both were likely contributing to her burst of attitude. "Is right here. Now, if you'll excuse me, I have a patient to see."

"I'll get Nick set in your room, Daisy." Tommy chuckled as she stormed up the stairs. He stepped closer to Loren. "Do yourself a favor, Loren. Don't ever go to Dominion Falls. The women there would flatten you in a second."

Loren's eyes narrowed. "They need to know their place."

"Oh, they do. Trust me on that." Tommy turned as a shadow darkened the doorway.

"Thank you for your assistance," Nick muttered as he approached. He dropped the four satchels and leather suitcase he'd been carrying. "I believe Daisy could well have found her way the twenty yards to the saloon without a guard."

"Not necessarily. You don't know this town. It's full of fools." Tommy glared once more at Loren before grabbing two of the bags. "You'll be next to us. Right this way."

Nick followed without argument. He remained silent until they'd entered the small room. "I'll take the floor. Dr. Pearson can have the bed. What of the children? Have they said anything?"

"I suggested they wait to tell their story until you were here so they wouldn't have to again. The boy, Jaybird, says almost nothing in English. He prefers Ute. The girl is more of a talker, but she trusts no white man, and mostly only talks to Leanne right now."

"So not much has changed since your initial telegram. Am I to assume the girl has come out of her ill state, then?"

"She has. I suggest we wait here a few minutes so Daisy might do her examination. We aren't sure if Jacob got his hands on her." Tommy's stomach turned at the suggestion.

Nick went so far as to flinch, a reaction rarely seen on his stoic brother. "How old is she?"

"We're guessing thirteen. The boy is about ten, and we're pretty sure he doesn't remember his real parents at all. Shivering Willow seems to, though." He recounted how the reverend mentioning her white name had caused the first asthma attack.

"And there are none of her blood remaining?" Nick pulled a small notebook from his pocket. "You did a thorough search?"

"I did ask for one. I'm still waiting on final word, but as of last I checked, there isn't anything on record." Tommy settled into the one chair the small room afforded. Unlike the room he and Leanne shared, this one didn't even have a table or a dresser. There was little doubt this room had one goal. "Even if they did, the children are too scared to acknowledge any white ties. I'm going to see if I have a few more strings to pull to get them to see their parents."

"Are you certain that is a wise decision?" Nick's eyes narrowed at his brother. His goatee did an odd twitch, unlike its usual eerily still nature. "Such a thing could make an already difficult situation impossible."

"Or they could hear from their parents own lips that it isn't safe for them there. They might accept that it's best they go. They won't believe us telling them that's what their parents said, they have to hear it for themselves."

Nick studied him quietly. "Who's idea?"

"Doesn't matter."

"I thought such a thing sounded more like an idea Leanne or our sister would come up with. I have had no communication with Jane since my departure, at which point she was fretting over the events here. What conclusion has she arrived at?"

"She's said to bring the children home—that we would find a home for them, somewhere."

"Which means if she isn't overrun by the idea they were raised by Indians, or cannot find another suitable home for them, she'll take them in."

"Cole always says she takes in too many strays."

"She is rather running out of room, and her apartment is but a year old."

"Sally's nearly an adult, and practically engaged. She might move out." Tommy knew Jane wanted no such thing. Sally had only been their ward for just over a year and a half. Jane wanted more time before Sally moved on. "Unless Jane finds a way to make her stay."

"She always does. She made all of us stay."

"Too true."

* * * *

Leanne hugged Daisy soon as she entered the room. "So good to see you. I've been frantic trying to do as we should."

"I'm sure you did just fine." Daisy returned the hug. "After all, Shivering Willow is awake and breathing better, or so I heard?"

Leanne nodded toward the table where the pair sat together sharing some crackers and honey. "I haven't been able to get them bathed beyond a sponge bath when Willow was unconscious. We were hoping this evening we'd manage it."

"It's all right." Daisy patted her hand, a smile set in place. Oddly enough, the smile didn't quite reach her yes. "I've done some exams in far worse conditions. They look well. How about some introductions?"

"Of course." Leanne guided her the rest of the way in the room. "Shivering Willow, Jaybird, I'd like you to meet my friend Daisy. She's the doctor Tommy and I spoke of."

They both eyed Daisy in a mix of doubt.

Leanne crouched before them. "I mean it. She's my doctor, too. I'd like it if you let her examine you and make sure you're healing well. Do you mind?"

Willow looked from Leanne to Daisy and nodded.

"Good." Leanne rose. "Who will go first?"

Jaybird shot out of his chair fast enough to block his sister's attempt to rise. "Me."

Daisy nodded. "All right. Why don't we move the screen in front of the bed? It'll give us some privacy, without blocking the sound if either of you gets nervous."

Leanne moved to grab the screen as Daisy had suggested. Jaybird seemed poised to protest, but Willow said something that appeared to soothe away his objection. Once Leanne had the screen in place she moved to the table with Willow. She spoke low, "I think the screen is more for your exam, sweetie. Do you want me in there with you? It can be scary."

Willow lifted her chin proudly. "I'm strong."

"Oh, believe me, I know. However, this is still…" Leanne took a shaky breath. She set a hand on Willow's as she leaned in close. "Did Jacob hurt you? Your clothes were ripped."

Willow's hand shook and she yanked it away.

"Daisy will be checking for any wounds. That's why I'm asking if you want me with you."

"Jaybird, he should not be alone."

"He can sit with Tommy and Nick. Maybe tell them what happened. Then we can have your turn if you're up to it."

Willow glanced at the screen, her brows pursed. "We tell, together."

"Then he can just sit with them."

Willow nodded and lowered her gaze. Her hand snaked back to Leanne's. The tight grasp she used nearly made Leanne flinch. "He tried."

"Tried, but didn't succeed?" Leanne breathed a sigh of relief at the nod. "Good. I will still be with you if you want."

Willow nodded again.

Jaybird emerged from behind the curtain. "Done."

Daisy followed behind. "He was very brave and strong. Tommy did an excellent job setting the break, I didn't have to fix anything. Otherwise, Jaybird is quite healthy. He received a few bumps and bruises from the ordeal, but they are all healing nicely." She dipped her hands in the basin.

As she washed herself thoroughly, Leanne rose. "I'm glad to hear it. Jaybird, how about I take you next door with Tommy and Nick? I promise I'll stay here with Shivering Willow."

"No." Jaybird dropped into a chair. "Not leaving."

Willow turned and barked a few words to him. His only response was to shake his head fervently. She sighed and nodded to Leanne. "He can stay, he's…"

Leanne smiled in understanding. "Of course he is. As long as he promises to stay on this side of the curtain. You two can speak through it if he gets worried. Is that acceptable?"

Rather than wait for her brother to answer, Willow rose and nodded. "Yes."

Daisy smiled over Jaybird's protest. "Don't worry. You were just back there with me, Jaybird. I'll do a little more of an exam with her, but I won't hurt her. She'll tell you herself. Bring the chair up to the curtain if you'd like. And Leanne will be with her, you both seem to trust her a little, right?"

Jaybird shrugged. The noncommittal agreement would have stung if Leanne hadn't understood. She lifted her own shoulders. "I suppose as much as they could trust any white man right now after all they've been through."

Willow followed them back to the bed willingly enough. By the time she sat, her breath wheezed again.

Daisy immediately set her stethoscope on the girls' back. "Where are her herbs?"

"Right here." Leanne pulled the bag off the bedside table. "We've been using them to steam, trying to be sparing as she only has so much."

Daisy examined the bag, then sniffed. "I asked Black Moon about what they might use before I left. Clearly he doesn't know this region as well as he does Colorado or Kansas, but he gave me some suggestions. They work well enough, at least they have for her life so we won't alter them too much unless she gets as bad as she's been."

Willow took the pouch Daisy handed her and breathed in the mixture a few times. As her breathing eased, she remained still while Daisy continued her surface exam. The bruises were checked, as was the tender rib they hadn't noticed because of her other symptoms.

When it came time for her to lie down and be examined, Leanne nodded to her. She lowered her voice, "Perhaps you should talk to him now, reassure him that you're all right before we start. I imagine Jaybird is worried you've been so quiet."

Willow took the hand Leanne offered once she'd laid down as Daisy requested. She swallowed hard, eying Daisy nervously.

"This won't hurt," Daisy reassured her. "You can speak to your brother."

Leanne used her free hand to grab Daisy's arm while Willow said something to her brother. "She says he tried but didn't hurt her. You don't have to be too thorough, do you?"

"I'll be gentle, and just make sure she's telling the truth. Don't worry."

Chapter 17

All four adults met in the hall after the examinations were complete. Leanne settled herself close to the door so she could go inside if she was needed. Daisy took up the opposite position, which left Leanne smack dab in the middle of the two brothers, Tommy and Nick.

Under normal circumstances back at home where things weren't so chaotic that would be a tricky position for her. In the here and now where there was so much going on, and things with Tommy were only beginning to find solid footing, the sibling rivalry had her perched on the razor's edge.

Leanne knew Nick had no interest in her beyond friendship, even if at the onset they may have dabbled in flirtations. Still, the ever-stoic-in-appearance Nick had a wicked streak that drove him to tease his older brothers endlessly.

In particular he had a bone to pick with Tommy, as he suspected Tommy had long known about Jane's pre-amnesia existence as a criminal.

She hoped to sway any tendency toward too much trouble by leaning Tommy's direction. Leanne spoke before either of the men could make a peep, "Willow was not raped."

Tommy released a gust of relief. "Then we need to find out what happened."

"I agree." Nick turned his attention to Daisy. "Can you begin the autopsies immediately? If we can extract a story from the children you might be able to corroborate."

"I'd suggest you start on Jacob," Tommy interjected. "It's pretty clear how Lucy died. I want to know what did Jacob in. Seemed his gunshot wound was minor, same with his head injury."

Leanne stepped between the two men. "They've been put on ice at the icehouse behind the telegraph office. The icehouse is right behind it. Would you like Tommy to accompany you just to be certain you're safe?"

Tommy curled his lip at the suggestion.

Daisy frowned. "I'm capable of taking care of myself."

"I know you are in most situations, Daisy. This is different." Leanne set her hand on Tommy's. "You know as well as I do how up in arms the town is over these children in the first place. They jumped to an immediate conclusion that the children are to blame for the deaths. How do you think they'll react to a doctor, a woman doctor no less, walking in and cutting on those deceased bodies?"

"Not to mention, I need to hear what the children have to say for myself." Nick stepped a little too close to her, his voice too pleasant. "You, on the other hand, can hear the information second hand."

Leanne didn't need to see Nick to guess at the smirk he carried in his eyes. Tommy's hands clenched into fists. She had to waylay the situation before it got out of hand at a very inappropriate time. "Tommy, you know I'd rather you were there. The children know you, but Nick has a point. Jane sent him for legal advice."

"He'll scare the children." Tommy nudged his chin at his brother. "That weird thing he does. It's unsettling. They'll never tell."

Leanne chuckled despite her attempts to waylay the tension between the men. "Be nice, Tommy."

Unlike Leanne, Daisy remained almost stoic at the exchange. She eyed Tommy. "You mean how he talks without his facial hair moving one iota? It can be rather disconcerting."

Leanne winked at Tommy. "I'm sure we'll manage. I'll be there with them."

Tommy frowned, but nodded. "Fine, but take these." From a pocket he withdrew the two beaded leather pieces the children's parents had given them at the reservation.

"Oh, heavens. In all of the chaos I forgot!" Leanne drew the pieces close, a knot in her gut unwinding. "These might help them open up a little. I'm not sure she truly believes we did meet their parents."

"I've been holding onto them until a good time. I thought this might be it." He squeezed her hand. "I'll get Daisy to the bodies. You'll tell me later what they say."

"Of course." Leanne gave him a peck on the cheek. She ignored his pointed grin at Nick before he walked away. Once the pair had disappeared she shook her head with a small sigh. "Why must you provoke him?"

"It amuses me in a world where little amuses me." Nick set his hand at the small of her back. "Shall we?"

"You are a terribly mean man sometimes, you be nice to the children."

"I'm offended. Have you ever seen me be mean to a child?"

She frowned, but glanced up at him. "I suppose not. Somehow Clara and Colton aren't bothered by you in the least. And you shouldn't be mean to your brother. What happened in the past is in the past."

"Maybe I'm just jealous he won the girl."

"Please. You weren't interested."

"No. He won you long ago when he went and got himself shot. You two are the fools that waited so long." He winked. "Now. The children?"

She pushed aside her rush of shyness at his accurate assessment of her relationship with Tommy to nod in agreement. "Of course, the children."

She pushed open the door to lead him inside. Willow and Jaybird were where they'd left them, sitting at the table, though neither had touched the food Leanne had left out for them.

Nick remained behind as she approached the table.

"Willow, Jaybird, I'd like you to meet Tommy's brother, Nick. He's very nice, and very smart." Leanne nodded to Nick, who approached. "Nick, this is Shivering Willow and Jaybird."

"Hello." He nodded to them both before he sat, his pad of paper before him. "Tommy told me a lot about you both. You're very brave, you know. What's happened to you is not fair."

Jaybird eyed Nick suspiciously, but Willow had little reaction either way.

"Before we start, I have something for you. Something from your parents." Leanne held out the leather pieces, smiling when their eyes lit up and they grabbed them. "Your Ma wanted you to have them. To remember."

While the two spoke quietly to each other in their language, Nick leaned in. "Are you sure that wasn't too soon?"

"They need something to cling to. It's been nothing but a nightmare since the army found their family. I didn't want to wait any longer." Leanne took a deep breath and turned back to the pair. "Shivering Willow? Jaybird? Can we talk about what happened out at the farm now?"

"Ma." Jaybird held the piece close. "See Ma."

"I don't know yet. Tommy is working on it. First thing we have to do is help you two to be left alone by the people here. We have to know what happened." Leanne set a hand on Willow's arm. "You said Jacob tried to hurt you."

Willow clutched the piece of leather tight in one hand, and grasped Leanne's hand with the other. She nodded quietly. "He came at night. Stared at me a long time."

Leanne closed her eyes, regretting that she hadn't taken more action when her instincts warned her about Jacob.

"I tried to not move, be invisible. I wasn't invisible, but I thought if I didn't move…"

"He might leave you alone," Leanne finished in a whisper. "Think you were asleep?"

Willow took a shaky breath, a gentle wheeze filling the air.

"Easy, Willow. Take your time, don't panic." Leanne smiled when Jaybird darted over to get Willow's pouch of medicine. "There you go. Thank you Jaybird."

Willow released Leanne's hand to return Jaybird's hug.

Leanne and Nick waited quietly for several minutes. When Jaybird protested the next time Willow opened her mouth, Leanne met Nick's gaze. She sighed and nodded.

"I know you're both scared, and don't trust us much." Nick shrugged. "Or at least, you don't trust me, you don't know me. But we need to know what happened. People think you killed Jacob and Lucy."

"No!" Jaybird scowled darkly at Nick. "Didn't."

"I believe you, and I know Leanne and Tommy believe you. We have to know what happened, though, so we can prove it. You had the gun when Tommy and Leanne found you, and I know you did everything you could to protect your sister." Nick had turned his full attention on Jaybird while he spoke. The pencil sat beside his notepad, any pretense of taking notes gone while he gave children his full attention.

Leanne squeezed Willow's arm gently. "After Jacob stood there for a while, what happened? Did he come for you?"

Willow nodded. "He grabbed me. Jaybird slept at first, but I fought. I fought, but he was strong and I was…"

"It's all right. It's over now." Leanne did her best to reassure the girl, but she knew she was still scared and vulnerable, sick as she was.

"I was able to scream, once. He hit me, and I panicked. I was scared. My clothes, they ripped. Jaybird. He went after him." Willow paused to take a few wheezing breaths. She breathed deep from her medicine bag.

Jaybird straightened and gave a proud lift of his chin. "I knocked him away. He did this," he lifted his arm, "pushed me down. I fell from the ladder."

"They were sleeping in the hay loft," Leanne muttered to Nick.

"I still fought. Willow could not."

"I tried," Willow whispered. "I could not."

"I kicked, he kicked back." Jaybird frowned. "He had her in barn, she tried to run when I fell. He caught her. She didn't have medicine."

Leanne had to fight to not clench her fists. She cleared her throat. "This was all in the barn?"

Willow nodded. "Then she came. The lady. He didn't see her, she hit him, hard. Big pan."

"The cast iron skillet we saw on the floor?" Leanne blinked a few times. "That had to at least make him stumble a bit."

"He fell. On me." Willow wrung her hands together. "Lady pushed him off. Told us to run, but I…I could not."

"Your breathing? The asthma?" Nick's questions were soft and quiet. At Willow's acknowledgement, he jotted another note on his pad. "But you have your bag?"

"Jaybird went to get it. I tried to move, but he woke, grabbed me. Lady kicked him, he grabbed her, knocked her down. They fought, I crawled away. They were screaming, yelling, I was scared. Jaybird helped pull me across yard. I thought man would come find us. So scared."

"*Bang!*" Jaybird slapped the table in emphasis, causing them all to jump. "Lady shot man. *Bang.*"

"You saw this?" Nick lifted his head. "How?"

"Not far. Pulling backwards. She shoot, he barely fall before he gets up." Jaybird became more animated the more he spoke. His vernacular showed he spoke English far less than his sister, but he got his point across well enough. "We lay flat, hope he not see us."

"So scared," Willow repeated barely above a whisper. "He took the gun from her."

"*Bang!*"

Leanne jumped again at Jaybirds' declaration. "He shot her. Did she move at all after?"

"No." Willow shook her head, her hands shook as she drew her medicine bag close again.

"He went into house. I tried to move faster, we did." Jaybird's leg bounced so rapidly the floorboards shook, but he kept talking through his sister's continued silence. "Then he came out. Had lamp. Yelled for us. We lay still, quiet, afraid he'd hear."

"I tried to be quiet, but I was making sound. Made me more nervous, louder. He stood in doorway for long time, we didn't know what to do." Willow reached for Leanne's hand. "He put down the lamp…and fell."

"Fell?" Leanne looked between the two. "Just like that?"

Both of the children nodded in synch. Jaybird's leg settled to stillness, the bright animation from his frightening tale fading into the serious mask Leanne was accustomed to seeing him wear. He leaned closer. "Fell down. We thought it was a trick. Shivering Willow couldn't make breath, not at all. I was scared, but I ran back to house. Silent like Pa taught me. Man moved hand, so I took gun and got sister safe. We moved slow, too slow, I thought he chased. Then you came, found us."

"And now you are safe. You will be." Leanne smiled at them both. "I know you do not believe white promises, but I will do all I can to make sure you are. You did very well telling your story. May Nick ask you any questions he has?"

"I don't have any—not right now. Maybe after Tommy and Daisy are done." Nick tucked away his notebook. "Would that be all right with the two of you?"

"Yes," Willow all but whispered.

"You look tired now." Leanne brushed her hand over Willow's soft hair. "Why don't you lie down while we wait? Jaybird, will you help your sister?"

The siblings moved behind the curtain they'd left in front of the bed.

Leanne took a shaky breath and lowered her head to her hands. "Oh my."

Nick rubbed her back gently. "They were very brave. Don't worry now. Soon as we hear from Daisy, I'll be ready for the marshal. There's no case here. We'll get them taken care of without any trouble."

"I hope you're right. They've had enough trouble for a lifetime."

"Yes they have."

Chapter 18

Once again they all gathered in the hall. Tommy did his best to follow the story as Nick and Leanne relayed it. He was too distracted by the scene he'd walked in on upon their return to the room. Nick with his arm around Leanne, comforting her.

Though Leanne had greeted him with a hug, Tommy was still annoyed with his brother and the smug twinkle in his eyes. Bastard was enjoying every minute of Tommy's frustration.

As Nick finished the story, Daisy nodded. "That sounds like a very truthful story based on what I learned in the autopsy. Lucy did die of the gunshot wounds. Jacob, however, died of a brain aneurysm. The blow to the head might have caused it to burst, or just the stress of the situation could have done it."

"A—what?" Leanne pursed her brows together in adorable consternation.

"Aneurysm. It's when the wall of an artery grows weak and the blood builds up in one area. Anything can cause it to burst," Daisy explained. "Brain aneurysms are almost impossible to detect until they've burst and caused a stroke. We know so little about the brain."

"Are you sure it was an aneurysm and not the blow to the head itself that caused the bleed?" Nick made notes on his pad through the whole thing.

"Well, the evidence shows it was an aneurysm. Again, it could have been the blow to the head that caused it to burst. There was not much blood beneath the actual impact area to indicate the blow caused a bleed itself." Daisy took a deep breath. "So that's that, then?"

Nick studied his notes, then closed the pad. "Should be sufficient to deal with the marshal. We'll be ready to go after the marshal is done with the children."

"What about the children? Will we be able to take them with us so Jane might find them a home?" Leanne frowned. "I did tell them we'd do all we could to make sure they were safe."

"That's my next order of business. I'll go meet with the reverend. McGonagall you said, right?" Nick focused on Leanne.

"Yes. He's very kind, I hope he doesn't object too strongly."

"I'm sure I can convince him." Nick set his hand on her elbow. "I'll go now. I don't think the marshal will be here until tomorrow, so I have time."

"Thank you." Leanne smiled bright and squeezed his arm. Tommy clenched his hands in silent protest of the affection. Leanne turned back to Daisy. "While we have time, will you come meet the twins and do their exams?"

"Of course." Daisy gathered her bag from the floor. "What of the other whore Tommy mentioned? Enid?"

"She hasn't given me her decision yet. If we spot her, I'll try to get her in the room as well. I'd rather that situation be done with anyhow." Leanne's voice faded as the pair moved down the stairs together.

Tommy turned to glare at his brother.

Nick paid him little mind. With a casual air, he dropped his pad into his pocket. He made a great show of straightening his jacket before he bothered with Tommy. "Thomas. Was there something else you required?"

"No." He could curse his own stubborn pride for keeping his answer so simple.

"Are you certain? Did you need me to repeat the tale the children told? You were rather distracted while Leanne and I spoke."

"I'm fine. I'm not the one that needs to take notes because I can't remember small details or direct lines like the rest of us." Tommy knew the jab was childish, but he couldn't help himself. "I'm going to go check on the children."

"All you've ever needed to do was request I back off. You instead resort to childish behavior and causing yourself to nearly lose her. If you wish to knock at someone's pride, take a look at your own." Nick's tone remained quiet and calm.

Somehow, though he knew Nick intended the opposite, the calm tone only riled Tommy more. "Excuse me?"

"Leanne. She cares a great deal for you, and you are apt to ruin it. You've bumbled on longer and more ineptly than our sister did at attempting a relationship. Jealous as you might be of our affections, it has been mere friendship for quite some time. The only one to blame for your delayed coupling is yourself."

Tommy's anger crumbled the moment Nick suggested he and Leanne were not courting in any fashion. He sighed. "I'm aware of this."

"Then do something about it." Nick stepped back so they were side by side. "If the children find it agreeable, Daisy and I will sit with them tonight. You and Leanne may have our room. We have no need for privacy anyhow."

"That's a generous offer. I'll have to see if the kids and Leanne mind." Tommy hoped neither of them would. Maybe he and Leanne could finally have a quiet minute again. Maybe figure out what they were going to do moving forward.

"Good. It's about damn time, too." Nick elbowed him in the ribs. "For a while I was certain you were being intentionally obtuse to give Jane fits. Then I realized it wasn't intentional, you were just obscenely oblivious to your own heart. It was quite painful to watch."

"Did you and Jane discuss this or something? You sound just like her."

"No. Jane and I do not have lengthy heart-felt discussions about your love life." Nick actually chuckled. "I think she has far too much to pester me about. Perhaps discussing you would have been a nice change of pace."

"I'm so upset you didn't think of it earlier." Tommy laced sarcasm into every word. "Does Jane pester you as much about finding yourself a woman of your own?"

"No." The humor dropped from his tone in the one syllable. "She still carries too much guilt to try to foist herself on me."

"Are you ever going to release her from it?" Tommy turned to face his brother, who maintained a stoic staring contest with the opposite wall. "She isn't Clara, and what Clara did was years ago."

"She is still Clara. Part of her is." Nick lifted his chin. "It is none of your business."

"It is my business. How bad do you need to hurt her to feel your pain is equaled? Jane isn't the one that told you to not desert, and did just the opposite while you lived through hell. That was young, naïve Clara. Jane has done nothing but love you and do her damnedest to make up for the past crime she didn't commit. Every time you deny her hope for forgiveness, you hurt her all the more. Let it go, Nicholas. Let the past go, and move into the future. If you can't, then leave Dominion Falls, because this isn't fair to you or Jane."

Nick blinked a few times, then pushed from the wall. "I must go speak to the reverend about the children. My offer still stands."

Tommy sighed as his brother took off. They'd been at odds over Nick's treatment of Jane from the start. Nick held a grudge and a half because their sister Clara had been insistent he not desert during the war, that there was life on the other side of the horrible pain, and had told him she'd always be there if he needed her—only to take off and disappear into the life that eventually turned her into Jane.

There were many times now Nick treated Jane well enough, but he let her carry a guilt that wasn't even her own over what Clara had done. They all knew the war had changed their brother in ways most of them couldn't understand. Still, the way he kept the pain so close was hurting himself and Jane deeper than either of them deserved.

Tommy shook off the dark thoughts and turned back to the room. Perhaps if he focused on the hope of some quiet time with Leanne he wouldn't seem so glum to the children. Those kids were too observant for him to go in without a smile on his face.

He took a deep breath, thought of Leanne, and entered the room. Only to find the children asleep on the bed.

He chuckled and took a seat, picking up a book as he did. Soon enough they would wake, and Leanne would return. Then he wouldn't need help putting his smile back on.

* * * *

On their way down to the room the twins were being held in, Leanne managed to snag Enid from the near-empty saloon. She'd have been worried if Loren weren't half-lying on the bar, eyes misty, almost drooling.

Enid confirmed Leanne's suspicions in a whisper, "He thought he'd be fine if he only had a little of his opium. He missed out earlier in all the excitement around them kids."

"Turns out even a little is too much." Leanne couldn't even act surprised by this. Beside her Daisy even went so far as to scoff. Leanne shrugged. "Anyone with half a brain would be aware, but I believe we've learned Loren is losing his brain to his indulgence."

"They always do," Daisy agreed.

Leanne unlocked the door and ushered the two women in. Nellie and Flo sat quiet on the bed, the conversation they'd been in when the women walked in dissipated.

Flo grinned. "I knew you'd be back. Nellie wasn't so sure."

"Neither of you were sure, but that's no matter now. I'd like you both to meet Dr. Daisy Pearson. She'd going to do your exams, along with Enid's." Leanne frowned at Enid's protest. "You haven't given me your answer, I concede as much. However, since Daisy is already here and you are as well, we might as well speed up the process and have your exam done now. At the very least you can be less concerned about your current state of health in the end."

Enid hesitated another moment before she nodded. "All right."

"You're really a doctor?" Nellie eyed Daisy from top to bottom. Doubt furrowed her brows.

"I am." Daisy didn't balk at the question, used to it as Leanne imagined she was. "I went to college and everything. My degree is back home, though, so you'll have to believe myself and Leanne—who has been under my care for a few years now."

"She is one of two doctors in Dominion Falls. And yes, she is a doctor." Leanne smiled at Nellie. "Why don't you go first? Flo, Enid and I will wait out in the hall."

Nellie clutched her sister's hand. Flo leaned in to whisper something to her sister. Their hands released moments later and Flo followed Leanne out of the room. She leaned against the wall with a smirk. "You know we're whores. Modesty isn't exactly required."

"I'm well aware, but a doctor's exam is different. I always require those are in private. Some matters don't need aired." Leanne shrugged. "So long as they prove trustworthy, I always afford my whores a measure of privacy and independence."

"Daisy one of your whores?" Flo didn't even show a flicker of a smile, the girl wasn't kidding. "That why she's allowed to be doctoring?"

"Daisy's definitely not one of mine. She's not a whore." At the pointed looks from both women, Leanne allowed the truth. "She was a whore for a few years, but has since left the business to resume being a doctor."

Flo snorted. "Of course she has."

"Excuse me?" Leanne frowned at the girl.

"Whores know whores, Miss DuBois. You aren't one, though you claim to be, and run a house of them. That lady?"

Flo jerked her thumb toward the room. "She's no lady. She's a whore—doctor or not."

The door, which had been cracked open, opened all the way to reveal Daisy and Nellie on the other side. Daisy's cheeks were flushed, her lips taut, but she said nothing. If anything, she avoided Leanne's gaze. "Flo, I believe you were next."

Leanne said nothing as the two disappeared into the room. Surely someone would know, the word would have made it around town. "She's courting Mike, the idea is ridiculous."

She had no idea she spoke aloud until Enid replied, "Flo's not wrong. I'm surprised you don't see it."

"Never tried to look for it. We're friends, I thought we were, or at least she's friends with Jane…" Whose brother Daisy was courting, or by all accounts at least. No, it was truly ridiculous. Leanne shook her head to regain focus. She turned to Nellie. "How did it go?"

Nellie simply shrugged, her eyes focused on the door. When Flo emerged a few minutes later, Leanne gestured Enid in. Nellie turned to Leanne. "Enid?"

"She's been a good help to the two of you, it was because of her that we learned the truth of your situation. Plus, she's been good enough to assist where we needed with the children. Just like the two of you, I promised to not add time to her contract, although unlike the two of you, I think she'll actually take me up on it." Leanne smiled. "She has plans after her two years. You two asked for a longer contract."

"More time means more money. She wants a husband, a so-called normal life. We don't." Flo shrugged. "No need for a man, we've had plenty. We just want enough to survive and leave the men behind."

"Fair enough." Leanne nodded. "I'm sure you aren't the first whores to feel that way. I've know a few that have done exactly as you want. I have your new contracts set and ready to sign."

"Contracts? Plural?" Nellie and Flo glanced at each other and back to Leanne.

"Yes. You are two separate people. Oh, Loren bought you as a matched set. Have you ever pleasured men separately?"

"Well sure. When one man can't afford, two go in together." Flo shrugged. "But we only got the same percentage either way."

"Well, you'll each get a greater amount should someone request the matched set, but you'll also have individual clients and income." Leanne studied them both. "And there is another matter we must discuss before we return to Dominion Falls."

The door opened then, and Enid slipped through before Daisy could finish opening. Leanne managed to block her exit, before she turned her attention to Daisy. "Well?"

"The twins show evidence of bruising from what they say is the banker. Otherwise, they are all acceptable health-wise. They'll need to learn to take better care of their parts, and will need regular checkups for a while. Lucky for them business is slow two thirds of the year." Daisy tucked her bag under her arm. "Now, if you'll excuse me."

"Daisy, wait." Leanne followed her to the end of the hall. "About what Flo was saying."

"I've been a whore, you don't need to explain anything to me, Leanne, or defend me." Daisy glared at her. "So let's leave it at that."

"I thought we were friends, I thought you and Jane were friends. You can talk to us, you know." Leanne studied Daisy. "Is what they said true?"

"Jane and I tolerate each other, make nice. We've never been friends, and it's none of your business. They're whores, poor, uneducated whores. I am not." Daisy turned on her heel and stormed up the steps.

Leanne frowned, wondering at Daisy's reaction. If it weren't true, would she have gotten so upset? If it were, why wouldn't she say so? All things considered, Leanne wasn't one to judge. Whoring was good money if done right.

She shook off the thoughts and turned back to the women down the hall. As she approached, Flo and Nellie watched her hopefully. She nodded to the twins. "Wait for me upstairs outside my room, second on the right, and we'll sign your contracts. Once they are signed you'll be officially free of this room."

When they disappeared up the stairs, Leanne focused on Enid. Enid shook her head. "I just gotta make it two years."

"And here you'd be slow enough except two or three times a year it doesn't matter so much. Except that it also means you won't be earning as much money." Leanne leaned against the wall. "I'll give you a greater cut of a greater price, I have regular clients, including ones that come in from Denver as they were regular clients there."

"Loren won't like it none."

"Do you really care?" Leanne's brows rose when Enid's head dropped. "You do."

"He wasn't always all that bad. Then the silver mines closed, and things got bad."

"Things probably aren't going to get better." Leanne set a hand on Enid's shoulder. "You said you have a plan. I can help you see it through. Nick can help us draft a contract that makes us both happy. All you have to do is say yes."

Enid took a shaky breath and nodded. "One more night to think. Loren needs help keeping the saloon up when he's like this."

"One more night. We'll be making plans to leave tomorrow and I need to know if you'll be joining us or not."

Enid nodded, then darted away.

Leanne sighed softly and dropped her head back against the wall.

Much as she'd enjoyed some quiet time with Tommy, brief as it had been, it would be good to get back home. Heber City had been little more than chaos since she'd arrived. She was ready for some peace and quiet again.

Chapter 19

Contracts were signed, and Leanne had tasked Nick with drafting another for Enid that she hoped would meet both their expectations. After a while Daisy had reappeared more like herself, with no hint of the anger she'd shown earlier.

Rather than try to deal with that in the midst of all they had going on, Leanne dropped the subject completely. Nick insisted they go out to eat, as they'd been trapped in the room for several days caring for the children. Under the agreement of the children, Leanne had acquiesced.

Sitting at a table in the small restaurant amid people, even those who eyed them now and then, bolstered Leanne's spirit enough that she ate heartily. Halfway through the meal, Tommy leaned forward. "Nick also offered to stay with the kids tonight, to let us use their room so that we might—sleep."

The hint of hesitation before the word 'sleep' drew Leanne's attention. She met his gaze and set down her fork. "Are you hinting at anything, Mr. Young?"

"Depends on if you want me to or not, I suppose." He grinned and took another large bite of his catfish. "Because we are lacking sleep, so I'll go with it."

"I'm surprised to see that the arrival of familiar people hasn't erased your vile behavior." She chuckled. As he ate more, she shrugged. "I'm certainly not offended by either suggestion, but we are both exhausted and have unfinished conversations. Not to mention we've both failed to do anything besides sleep in the past."

"Why is that?"

"I don't know. Why is that?"

He slowed down his eating as she dove back in. "You're afraid."

"So are you."

"Not afraid." He pushed around his beans, a frown lingering. "Exactly."

"And you don't want to piss off my brother, but Cole likes you, so I doubt that would happen."

"Unless I screwed everything up again. He'd never forgive me."

"True." She scooted her chair closer. "Then again, I'm not looking for marriage or babies or a houseful of strays, or even a house and an illegitimate, scandalous relationship. It's hard to mess up something like that."

"What even is that?" He chuckled. "Sounds like what we already do—with a few extra benefits. Is that enough? What if you change your mind?"

"I am no spiritualist. I can't predict the future." She set her hand on his arm and leaned close. "I have an idea."

"All right, share."

"How about we take Nick up on his offer. See where the night leads. And then tomorrow we do the same. I've never been in any relationship with any man. You've been in a failed marriage and nothing since. Why must we choose anything?"

"No pressure."

"Maybe part of our problem has been the pressure. From Jane, Cole, half the town watching us…and you mistakenly believing anything was going on between Nick and I."

"You didn't dissuade that in any way."

"It was fun to watch you sweat." She met his gaze. "It let me know you were still interested, even if you didn't act on it."

"Wicked woman." He nudged her shoulder. "Finish eating. We'll take a walk before we go check on the kids and then head to bed."

"Sounds like a great plan." She had no trouble finishing her meal, reinvigorated by the positive turnaround things were taking. On the walk she once again dove into the tale of how she'd first met Cole. "He showed up at our homestead mad as anything I've seen, and I'd seen our Pa mad. He was ready to rip Pa to shreds, but Pa wasn't there, and instead he found me."

"What did he have to say?"

"Just like that, he wasn't angry. He didn't say anything though, he paled and turned around and walked away. I told Ma about it, but she didn't know it was him until he showed up again a couple of weeks later." She brushed aside a stray lock of hair. "He brought me a rag doll. I still have the thing. He talked to Ma a long time, but I was too busy playing with the doll to have any idea what they talked about."

"Were things different then?" He wrapped his arm around her waist and kept her close.

"For a time. Pa didn't come around much, but Cole came by every couple of weeks until Ella got pregnant—which was the same time Ma had Alma. Pa was more angry than before. He didn't want another baby, he got furious when she was pregnant, and stayed that way."

"Cole had other brothers and sisters, right?"

"Two brothers and a sister. They've long since died in a fire, probably one Pa set. I wasn't around then." She leaned into him. "Alma was born blue, they thought she was dead, but somehow she lived. She wasn't much right after. She wouldn't ever calm down if there was anyone around. Only me and Ma, and Cole when he came by, could touch her. It didn't take long to figure out something wasn't right. She didn't act like normal babies, she hardly ate, almost starved to death. Cole got his hands on a bottle so we could get her to eat more."

When she shuddered Tommy slowed their pace and led her to the bench outside the telegraph office. "What?"

"Pa already hated her. When she proved so different he tried to drown her in the creek. She was so little. Ma fought Pa to save Alma, but I ran to get Cole. He near killed Pa, they both got beat up bad." She could still remember the deep bruises on Cole's face. He'd been upset that Ella would know something happened, and he couldn't tell her what.

"When did he send you away?"

"It wasn't until a few months later. Lydia had died, Cole was…so tired, so sad. Ma had learned Pa was going to send Alma to an asylum. She was barely a year and a half old. Cole seemed to come back to himself when he found out. He helped us get to Indiana, made sure we were taken care of. Even when Ella died, he sent us money real regular."

"And the rest, as they say, is history. I know the rest of what he did for you, and how he is the reason you are the virgin madam."

She smiled, glad for the distraction from the sad turn of the conversation. "Yes. Only Cole would think to hire his sister as a whore, and make sure she remained a virgin. Not to mention help get her established as a madam in a high-class whorehouse in the next town at his own expense. Only one bad thing about that."

"Oh?"

"I'm to blame for him taking Graham as a partner. The cost of shuttling me off to Denver cost him a good year's profit."

"That is a bad thing. Although Graham has turned over a new leaf in recent years it seems." He rose, and tugged her along with him. The mood of the conversation turned as they went home, thanks to Tommy infusing some humorous stories along the way.

Back at the room they made sure the children were okay, but at Tommy's gentle insistence they left for the smaller room next door.

Inside, he pulled her close. Nerves made her stomach jump and she took a shaky breath.

His lips brushed hers in a gentle kiss. "I thought we were just seeing where it leads?"

"Nervous is all."

"Me too."

She chuckled softly, the butterflies in her stomach easing somewhat at his admittance. "You are? Really?"

"Hm-hm." He kissed her neck gently, the rough texture of his beard brushed along her skin, setting off tingle of excitement down her belly. "You know just enough to have expectations."

She sighed as he continued a trail of kisses along her jugular. "I clearly know nothing. So I can expect nothing."

"Why do you say that?" He paused to meet her eyes.

"Because I've never felt the jolt of excitement I just got at your touch."

A smile broke across his features. "Good to know."

"Just one thing." Her stomach did another little nervous flip, but it was quickly counteracted by the shiver of goosebumps that rose as he brushed his fingers along her arms.

"What's that?"

"Forget nerves, just don't stop."

"Yes ma'am."

* * * *

The next morning Tommy woke with a warm, supple body lying flush against his. He opened his eyes to blonde hair. Memories of their intense night flooded back. They'd taken things slow, but damned if it hadn't been amazing anyhow, at least for him.

His worries were interrupted by a shift in the woman beside him, enough to wake back up parts of him she was probably too sore to be happy to see this morning. She moved again and he groaned. "You'd best stop that."

"Hm?" When he backed away to avoid further squirming contact from her, she turned her head, the adorable pucker back between her eyebrows. "What?"

"Good morning, beautiful."

"Flattery so early, but why did you," She rolled toward him and her eyes opened wider, "Oh."

He chuckled low. "You keep squirming and I'll be eager to start again, but that little wince tells me you're a mite sore."

"Oh dear. I should have known that." A small chuckle emerged. She glanced his way and the laughter billowed forth. "I should have known that, shouldn't I?"

He joined her laughter. "As a well-established and profitable madam, yes. Probably."

"It's not a bad soreness." She sighed and rolled to face him, the muslin slipping free of her long legs to reveal the delicious swirl of her hips. "But it is there. It might be a few hours before I am ready to try again."

"Try? You succeeded." He set his hand on hers where it lay on the pillow he'd abandoned. "Other than the obvious, were you…"

She opened her eyes again and met his gaze. A slow, seductive smile crept across her features. "I might curse my brother for protecting me so long I was afraid to try."

"But there is something to be said for all you learned in that time. You weren't afraid to experiment once you got started."

"Jane is right. Men are all pigs." She smacked his hand, but a deep yawn cut off her laughter. "Oh, why did you wake me so early?"

A rooster crowed somewhere outside, and several dogs barked in response. He glanced toward the window where only a hint of light hit the lacey curtain. "It's not so early."

"No whore worth her salt gets up before ten in the morning."

"You're no whore."

She grinned. "After what we did last night? Twice?"

"That doesn't make you a whore." He kissed her temple. "But fine, sleep. I have to prepare for the marshal's arrival."

"Oh. The children."

He set a hand on her shoulder when she began to rise. "They'll be fine. I'll check on them. If there's any problems I'll wake you. Until then, get your rest."

She mumbled a protest as her eyes drifted shut again.

He climbed over her, careful not to touch any of the exposed skin for fear that one touch would make him stay longer. Much as he wanted to, they had plenty to do today. God willing they'd be on the stage back home by the next day and there was plenty to do before that.

After he'd pulled on some clothes, he yanked the door open only to find Nick there with his hand raised to knock. Nick lowered his hand, and with a peek in the room released the unfamiliar sound of his deep laughter. "About damn time."

"Shut your trap." Tommy shoved him into the hall as he finished slipping on his suspenders. "What are you doing up so early?"

"You never sleep past dawn, I figured you wanted an early start." Nick paused outside the room with the children. "They're still asleep, but if you care to look in on them, let's do so. The marshal is expected around noon according to his last wire. He was in the next town and riding in rather than waiting for the stage."

"Good. Do we have a name?" Tommy peeked into the room to check on the children. They were asleep in the bed, and Daisy still dozed on the blankets they'd spread on the floor. He shut the door quietly. "Let's get everyone some breakfast so we have it before they rise."

"Marshal's name is Paul Binder."

"Really?" Tommy patted his brother's shoulder. "Well that might be a stroke of luck we can handle right now. I'd like to head home by tomorrow with all the kids and whores in tow."

"How, exactly, is that a stroke of luck?" Nick kept pace with him easily down the street to the restaurant.

The smell of hash hit them while they were still two doors down. Tommy's stomach started rumbling on the spot. He glanced at his brother. "He's a former Pink, too. We worked together on a case we took up north."

"That doesn't mean it's a stroke of luck. You can be a real ass when on a case."

"Good point."

"So?" Nick stopped him at the door. "Is it really a stroke of luck? Or am I going to have to work hard to get him over your shortcomings?"

"Relax. It is a stroke of luck or I wouldn't have said it. Paul's no fool, and he'll easily be able to see what the right thing is. Now I need to eat."

"You always need to eat," Nick muttered.

"Well, that's not all I need to do anymore, and I need energy for the other." Tommy glanced at his brother. "Are you ever going to get out of your crazy head and find a woman?"

"We aren't discussing this."

"At least find a whore you can tolerate. It might help you get rid of some of that never-ending anger you carry around. You're driving your family crazy, you know."

"Says the man who skirted around taking the next step with Leanne all this time. You're yellow, always have been. Odd for a Pinkerton."

Tommy chuckled and shook his head. "You are so easy to rile. This should be a fun day, even more so than I expected. Good to know."

"You aren't funny."

"Actually, I am. Leanne agrees, too. So that's saying something."

"Ass."

Chapter 20

After everyone had eaten, Tommy went back into the room he'd shared with Leanne the night before. She still lay on the bed, her lashes fluttering with dreams he hoped included him. He knelt beside the bed and held the plate of hash level with her face.

Her nose twitched once, twice, then her eyes blinked open. She smiled. "Ah, what a nice thing to wake up to. Food, and the man I spent the night with. A girl could get used to this—you know, if she didn't have a business to run and all."

He kissed her temple. "So long as you are only running the business and not participating, I can handle this not happening every day."

"Oh my, jealous already? I haven't even done anything wrong yet." She accepted the robe he handed her and slipped it on as she emerged from the bed.

"Call it pre-emptive."

"I'd call it insecure." She scooped some hash into her mouth. "Then again, you are a Young so that seems impossible."

"On a totally separate subject." He didn't want her to keep harping on his insecurities. "The marshal is due to arrive in a couple of hours."

"Oh?" She paused with another spoonful halfway to her mouth. "Then I should get ready."

"Eat first, clothes later."

"You just want to see my legs more."

"It sure doesn't hurt." He chuckled as she ate more. "But you need sustenance. We're going to have a busy day."

"And a busy night after?"

"Depends on if my brother agrees to watch the children again."

"Mm, good point." She scarfed down the rest of the food. "That was delicious. Or I was starving. Perhaps both."

"Probably both." He held out his hand. "Let's go see the children, make them presentable, and ourselves. Paul will be here soon enough."

"Paul?"

"The marshal. I worked with him on a case some time back."

"So you know the marshal?" She followed him to the door. "That's good, right?"

"I sure hope so. I think we'll be ready to head home by tomorrow."

Leanne paused outside the door. "The children?"

"I talked to the reverend." Nick approached from the area of the stairs, a glass of whiskey in hand. "He agrees that you and Thomas have shown enough care to see the children find an appropriate home. Everything is in order, so long as the marshal clears them."

"Then I need to corner Enid and get her to either sign or agree to stay." Leanne frowned. "I do hope she chooses to go. Loyalty is a good thing except when it's at your expense."

"You can't make the choice for her, you know." Tommy nudged her. "She's got a good head on her shoulders. Makes me think she'll make the right choice."

"Well I hope so for her sake." She straightened her shoulders. "Anyhow, I'd best get dressed and check on the children before we meet with the marshal."

"How about we meet Paul at the stage and bring him back here? That way you can sit with the children a while, explain to them about where we're going." Tommy smiled. "It's been over twelve hours since you've seen them. Go on ahead. We'll be back in a bit with more food and the marshal."

Leanne relaxed. "Good. I like that plan."

"Any requests?"

"Surprise me." Leanne smiled, then gasped. "Wait. They'll ask about their parents. You said you'd try to arrange a meeting."

"Yes, I did work that out. We were distracted last night." Tommy grinned when her cheeks grew warm. "After everything is handled here with the marshal and the whores we'll head out that way. Work for you?"

"So long as it isn't too late." She nodded. "We'll see you soon."

Before she got the doorknob turned, Tommy planted a kiss on her cheek. He winked then led his brother back downstairs.

Leanne couldn't stop her smile if she'd tried. She'd never admit it to Jane, but she fairly skipped her way into the room. Daisy sat curled in a chair by the window, but the children both rushed to meet her.

After she'd given hugs to them both, she excused herself to dress behind the curtain. When she emerged she took a seat. "Why don't you two join me? I'd like to tell you about what's going to happen over the next few days."

Both children sat, Jaybird didn't focus on her, though. His gaze lay on the remaining apple with intensity.

Leanne chuckled. "You want it? Go ahead, I'm sure Tommy will bring more when he brings our lunch. What about you, Willow? Would you like some crackers and honey? I think we have a few pieces left."

Willow nodded. "Yes."

Glad the pair had healthy appetites still, Leanne handed over the goods. Once they were eating happily, she leaned her arms on the table. "In a couple of hours Tommy is going to bring the marshal by. Don't worry too much, he just wants to meet you."

"Will we—have to tell again?" Willow spoke with clarity again, only a hint of her wheezing remained. The color had returned to her face for the most part, until the idea struck that she'd have to tell the story again.

"No, I don't think you will, that's why Nick took all those notes."

Willow breathed a sigh of relief. Jaybird resumed crunching on his apple.

"Tomorrow we plan to leave on the stage, the whole lot of us. You two, Tommy, Nick, Daisy and myself, along with three other ladies, including Enid. We'll be heading to where we're from, in Colorado." Leanne set her hand on Willow's. "We're still hoping to get you to see your parents before then, would you like that?"

Both the children straightened in their seats, a mix of eagerness and tears on their faces.

"But that's at least a few hours away. In the meantime, would you like to hear about Dominion Falls? I think you're going to like it there."

Willow didn't even glance at her brother, she nodded. "We will listen, but we won't go unless Ma and Pa say."

"Of course."

* * * *

Tommy peeked out of the curtain to scan the surrounding area for signs of the arriving marshal. According to the telegram that had been sent, he was expected to arrive around two. According to Tommy's pocket watch, it was now quarter past.

Leanne had told the children much about Dominion Falls and the people, namely the children around their ages, that they'd meet. Both the children had listened intently, but said nothing and had little reaction.

For now, Leanne distracted them with a game of jack stones she'd grabbed at the mercantile. He was worried about her attachment to the children, especially if things didn't work out for them back home.

Movement in the distance pulled his attention back out the window. A single rider drew closer to town. Tommy cleared his throat. "I'm going to head out for a little while."

Leanne paused in her throw to sit straighter. "Is he here, then?"

"I think so. I'll grab Nick on my way out. Will you all be all right here?"

"We'll be fine." She rose to follow him to the door.

He pulled her gently into the hall and closed the door most of the way. "I'll make sure Paul knows all the details before he gets here. Hopefully he won't need to really mess with the kids too much."

"Good. I'm not sure how much they should have to handle. They're strong, but they are still only children."

"Hey." He tucked a finger under her chin. "You sure you're not too attached?"

"What? No. Of course not. I'm simply worried for them. I'm sure I made it clear that I have no intention of having children in any way. I don't have a lifestyle for it, nor would I be any good at it."

"Your brother took you in under worse circumstances."

"And lied and manipulated to do so." Despite her protest, she smiled at the reminder. "And I am not my brother or your sister. They are the ones that like to take in strays."

"Good. I wanted to be sure. You know if Jane caught any whiff of attachment, she'd use it against you so she wouldn't be tempted."

She laughed. "I'm well aware of Jane's tactics. Now go on. We don't want anyone else getting to the marshal first. By the way, have you seen Daisy?"

"Not since this morning." He gave her a quick kiss on his way to the stairs. "I'll let her know if you're looking for her should I see her."

"Thank you." She waved, a pleasant flush to her cheeks after the kiss.

He quick-stepped it down the stairs. On his way out he tapped Nick's shoulder. His brother needed no other prompting to finish his scotch and follow him out. Tommy placed his hat on his head soon as they got into the sun.

Both of them strode through town at a quick pace, and managed to reach the edge of town a few minutes before Paul got there. As the horse and rider came into view, they slowed. Laughter carried through the air. "Well, I'll be the son of an uncle. Thomas Young. Why am I not surprised you're tangled in this nonsense?"

Tommy met Paul's laughter with his own. When the tall, skinny man dismounted, Tommy offered his hand. "Paul. You would not believe the sort of nonsense I find myself tangled in on a regular basis."

"I would. I've met you." Paul clapped him on the shoulder. Tall and thin though he was, he carried a wiry strength that caught most people off-guard. "Glad you're here, though. The wire I got from someone here seemed awful extreme. I trust you got details."

"We have. This here's my brother, Nick. He's a lawyer and managed to get everything together. We had an autopsy done, and spoke with the children to get their story."

"Then why am I here?" Paul shook Nick's hand.

"Townsfolk have a grudge against the Indians, and these children were raised by an Ute family. They were found when the tribe was captured and brought to the reservation. The Army wouldn't let them stay with their family since they were white." Tommy folded his arms across his chest. "They've been met with nothing but contention since they were brought to town."

"Here's the file. I made this copy for you." Nick handed over a stack of papers. While the man hadn't the memory of the rest of his family, he could write faster and neater than any of them. "It seems to me it's pretty cut and dry. I'll leave you to decide that, though."

"Thank you." Paul took the files and slid them into his saddle bag. "Let's get somewhere I can look them over."

"We can head to the saloon." Tommy led the way. "How long have you been marshal?"

"Going on two years now. I left the Pinkerton's about five years ago, took a few years off. Tried to have a life. That didn't work for me, so I took this job." Paul glanced his way. "What on earth are you doing back in these parts? Thought you gave up finding your sister some years back. Didn't figure you'd be back to Utah."

"Our sister has been found," Nick snapped.

"Sort of," Tommy corrected. "She's in Colorado now. Has complete amnesia up until a few years back. She went through a mess of something, and so we're just glad to call her Jane now. At least she's back, in a way."

"Amnesia, eh?" Paul pursed his lips. "Interesting. You'll have to tell me the story sometime."

"I will, so long as you tell me about the life that didn't work out."

"Don't imagine it's much different than yours. After life as a Pink, things aren't the same."

"Agreed." Tommy glanced at Nick, who'd resumed his glowering countenance.

"What are you doing now?" Paul pulled his attention back. "You aren't living a normal life, are you?"

"In some ways, yes. In others, not so much. I'm a deputy in Dominion Falls, and hotel manager for The Hangman's Inn, which Jane owns and runs." Tommy shook his head. "Somehow I've been there around two years solid."

"Got a woman?"

"Just."

"Really?" Paul paused to tie his horse to the hitching post. "Didn't think you would after your divorce."

"Well, this isn't your typical woman, so it's different."

"Now I am intrigued. But first," he withdrew the files from the saddlebag, "let's deal with business."

"Finally." Nick stormed back into the saloon.

"What's his deal?" Paul nudged his chin to the swinging doors.

"War. The deal with our sister. It's complicated." Tommy clapped him on the back. "Come on, I'll buy you a drink and you can read. You still drink beer?"

"I'll take a gin, actually."

"Gin it is."

"So tell me about this woman."

Tommy chuckled and led him into the saloon. "You'll meet her soon enough, and she just became my woman, so be nice."

"That so?"

"She's a madam for a high class whorehouse back home."

"Well, damn. You're a lucky man."

"Damn straight."

Chapter 21

Leanne rose to her feet soon as the door opened. After days in the room, the children were becoming increasingly restless. "Tommy. We have to take these poor things outside. They're going mad being trapped in here."

"Hello to you too." Tommy smirked as he held the door open. A slim man walked in behind him, a satchel in one hand and his hat in the other. "Leanne, this is Paul Binder."

"Oh, sorry." Leanne's nerves jumped at the sight of the marshal. She gathered her wits enough to extend her hand. Paul immediately shuffled his hat to accept her shake. "It's good to meet you, Marshal Binder. I trust you've already read the details."

"I have. We spent some time downstairs going over everything before we came up." Paul's smile was warm and set her at ease. "I don't think there will even be need to talk to the children any further. They've been through enough far as I can see."

"That's wonderful to hear. Shivering Willow, Jaybird, why don't you come say hello to Tommy's friend, Mr. Binder?" She turned to the bickering children. "He's going to see to it we can be on our way tomorrow, hopefully."

Both children stopped mid-argument to stare at Paul. Willow rose slow, but only moved as far as Leanne's side. She nodded at the gentleman, her face stoic.

"Hello, Shivering Willow." Paul nodded to him, then glanced behind her to Jaybird. "And Jaybird, I hear you were your sisters' hero."

Jaybird pursed his lips, but couldn't hide his smile at the comment.

Paul set down his satchel. "I'll deal with the town this afternoon. First, Tommy says you all are hoping to go out to the reservation."

Willow clutched Leanne's skirts tight at the mention of the reservation. "Ma. Pa."

"That's right, Willow. Tommy is trying to see it happens." Leanne ran her hand along the tense girl's back. "Tommy?"

"I'll let Paul take the lead on this. Although..." Tommy turned his attention to the children. "Why don't I take you both next door? Enid brought up a checkerboard and offered to teach you both how to play."

"Checkerboard?" Willow's brows pursed.

"It's a game." Leanne smile. "One I think both you and your brother will like. It's easy enough to learn. Maybe, just maybe, we'll have time to go fishing after the adults talk, like I suggested earlier."

Willow hesitated, but then nodded. "All right. Don't forget. Ma. Pa."

"I promise we won't forget. Go on. Tommy?" She urged the children toward him. "Speaking of Enid. Has she said anything?"

"Nick is in with her now getting everything signed. Then, with your permission, he'll take care of Loren since we have so much planned for our afternoon." Tommy smirked. "Wouldn't want to step on the toes of an accomplished business woman, after all."

She knew he was teasing her for her snit when he'd tried to speak for her after they'd first arrived. If there hadn't been another adult present she might have stuck her tongue out at him, but instead she simply nodded. "That'll be fine."

Paul took a seat as the others left the room. "It's good to meet you, Leanne. Tommy speaks quite highly of you."

"Then I am flattered. Tommy doesn't speak highly of many people."

"Agreed."

"Would you care for a drink?" She offered before she took her own seat.

"No, thank you. I had some refreshment downstairs." He gestured to the seat across from him. "So you run a brothel?"

"I do, with six high-class girls working for me—well, nine once we return home. I used to run the Bonne Nuit in Denver."

"The Bonne Nuit. I've heard of that place. A few of my friends spoke very highly of your business. Why did you leave? Denver must be more profitable than Dominion Falls."

"That's personal, I'm afraid."

"Not Tommy?"

"What? Oh, heavens no. We were merely friends when I decided to sell the business and move to Dominion Falls." Leanne curved her lips in a well-practiced coy smile. "It would take far more than a man to get me to do anything, much less give up my business. Either way, I do well enough back home."

Paul chuckled low. "Fair enough. How did you become a madam?"

"I was an orphan, became a whore, and was good enough to get out and start my own place." Granted, it was with a load of help from her brother, and some very talented whores. Still, her business acumen made it grow into what it was. "Simple as that."

"One thing I've learned, Leanne—nothing is ever simple as that." He winked.

"Fair enough." Amusement bubbled under the surface, but she kept it well in check. The man was friendly and infinitely charming. She had a feeling he was every bit as clever as Tommy, and didn't dare to try to play him in any way. "So what is it that you two felt the children could not be around for?"

"I had an idea involving the children's parents." The door opened, and Paul nodded to Tommy. "I just started telling her about my plan."

"Good. I'd hoped you'd start." Tommy took a seat near Leanne. "Paul thinks we can not only get the kids to see their parents, but we might be able to get them into a better situation."

Leanne frowned. "How so?"

"There are a couple of options. I know of a reservation closer to where you live where the treatment isn't so dreadful." Paul leaned forward. "We could move them there, and they'd be closer to the children."

"Are there any Ute there?" Leanne shook her head. "And what reason would they have for arriving? I don't assume that interlopers from other tribes are appreciated even on the likes of a reservation. They probably wouldn't ever agree."

"There aren't Ute there," Paul acknowledged.

"They won't go." Leanne turned to Tommy. "You saw how they acted simply to our presence. We put them in danger by even going. Why would they go where there are no other Ute? Without good reason?"

"Calm down." Tommy set his hand on hers. "That was just one suggestion. I have the same concerns as you. We just thought perhaps being closer to the children would be good."

"They wouldn't ever get to see them hardly anyhow. This afternoon is…" Leanne's heart skipped a beat. "It's likely goodbye for them."

Tommy squeezed her hand in reassurance. "The other option is to get another soldier in here in charge of the reservation. Soldier transfers happen all the time. Superintendent Tait is fair enough in his thoughts on the Indians, but he can't be everywhere at all times."

"Unfortunately, he doesn't always catch the abuse. He maybe visits once or twice a year at most." Paul sighed. "However, if we can get better guidance over this reservation it'll at least put your mind at ease leaving here."

Leanne nodded. "They've had their children taken away. I'd hate to see anything worse happen to them now."

Paul frowned. "Unfortunately, there isn't much worse than that."

* * * *

Leanne couldn't help but smile at the sight before her. After all the bickering in their room, the two children were alternately laughing. Paul had taken to showing them a few tricks he'd mastered with a trundling hoop.

Willow seemed happy enough to watch the tricks while she kept her hoop rolling for a surprisingly long time. Jaybird had other ideas, and tried to mimic Paul's every trick. The consequences of which left him tangled in his own hoop on a few occasions.

Leanne's relief that they'd gotten the children out of the small room echoed into her bones until she felt the exhaustion of the past week tugging on her. A hand on her shoulder pulled her attention away from her vigil of the children.

Tommy leaned close, a warm smile on his features. "It's good to see them laughing."

"I wasn't sure it was possible. Your friend is good with children."

"Too bad he never had any of his own. Always knew he would be good."

"Really? He appears to be a natural."

"Grew up in an orphanage, been around plenty of kids. He didn't get out of there until he turned sixteen and got himself a job far away." Tommy bumped her shoulder with his. "While they're distracted, I'm going to head on out to the meeting point early. Talk to the parents a bit before we take the kids to them."

"Good idea. I'd like them to know what's going on before the children have their chance. Be careful, please." She knew they weren't meeting the children's parents on the reservation this time, but that didn't mean the situation was much safer. "We won't be far behind."

"Yes ma'am." He kissed her temple. Without further ado, he hopped into the saddle.

His hoofbeats hadn't come close to fading when the laughter stopped abruptly nearby. Leanne turned to find both children staring at Tommy's departing back. She circled the wagon to where they stood. "Are you two ready to head out to see your parents?"

They both turned to meet her gaze. Neither of them said a word, or smiled, or anything. Three heartbeats later they scrambled into the wagon quicker than she'd seen them move yet.

Paul chuckled. "I think they thought you might have been fooling, or that it might not happen." He bent to pick up the scattered hoops.

"I can't say that I blame them." Leanne followed them to the wagon.

She'd hardly grabbed the side when Paul offered his hand. He grinned. "I'd rather leave hoops in the street than allow a lady to get into a wagon without assistance, even if she is infinitely capable of helping herself."

"I'm not certain if that makes you a gentleman or untidy and careless."

"Perhaps a bit of both." He aided her into the carriage. Before he joined her he did gather the hoops and toss them into the back of the wagon with the children. Once he'd climbed in, he winked. "Or just a gentleman."

She took the reins, relieved to see he didn't fight her on control of the wagon. Although eventually she'd need direction to where they were meeting the soldier and Indians, she needed something to do.

Paul filled the ride with mindless conversation and directions on where to turn. Though the children remained silent behind them, he spoke to them as much as he did Leanne. She kept the ride slow as possible to give Tommy time to do as he needed, but the anxiety of the two young ones behind her quickened their pace.

Soon as Tommy's horse came into view, chaos erupted. Shivering Willow let out a shriek. With her brother hot on her heels, she leapt over the side of the moving wagon.

Leanne tugged on the reins and kicked down the brake, but they'd already stumbled to their feet and raced off. She sighed and propped the reins on the dash. "Well, I hope Tommy finished what he needed to."

"I'm sure he's done what was needed." Paul patted her arm. "Why don't you remain here? This could be difficult. I know you've grown attached to them."

"Which is why I will be there, difficult or not." Leanne got herself out of the wagon before Paul could offer assistance. She dashed around the bend, and almost smack-dab into Tommy.

A short distance away the couple they'd met only a few days before were dealing with the children. Directly behind them, and right next to Tommy, soldiers hovered with hands on weapons. As if the children or their parents cared one way or another about stirring trouble right then.

Tommy acknowledged her with a short nod. When he spoke, he kept his tone low. "I told them our plans. They've agreed that it's best the children go."

"And our other point of discussion?" Leanne didn't dare bring up the idea to transfer them or get a new soldier in charge with the soldiers hovering so close.

"It will happen."

Leanne merely nodded. Before her Willow and her parents were in a deep discussion, and though the woman kept a stoic expression as best as she could, Willow did little to hide her tears. Now and then Jaybird piped up a strong word or two, but their parents only shook their heads.

The knowledge that this would be a goodbye for them, did little to compare to the actual event of the matter. Leanne's heart ached as every attempt to urge the children back their way ended with another protest from the children.

When their mother finally cast a pleading look their direction, Tommy's hand landed at the small of her back. They drew closer, and as they did the children grew quieter. Both parents whispered what appeared to be reassurances.

Leanne stopped in front of their mother and offered a single nod. "I assure you, they will never forget you. We will find them a place where they are allowed to remember and speak of you."

The woman offered a single nod in return. She pressed her forehead to each of the children's before she pushed them toward Leanne and Tommy. The tears on her cheeks were silent testament to the depth of her pain.

Their father backed up next to his wife. With one more nod to Tommy, he turned his wife and they walked back to the nearby soldier.

Willow whimpered, her shoulder jerked free of Leanne's grasp. Jaybird took two whole steps. Both quiet protests ceased as quick as they'd begun. Willow turned tear-streaked cheeks up to face Leanne. "We go."

"All right." Leanne smoothed down the hair that had broken free of Willow's braids. "We'll go."

Willow held tight to her brother's hand, but didn't rush ahead. She kept one hand on Leanne's arm so tight Leanne feared a bruise. Willow turned to look behind once more before they rounded the bend. Soon as their parents were out of sight, the grip on Leanne's arm eased.

Paul frowned as they approached. "Why don't I take the horse back, you all take the wagon?"

"Thank you, Paul." Tommy clapped him on the shoulder. His features didn't hold as much of the underlying joviality Leanne had grown accustomed to. Lines that hadn't been there a few hours before creased his forehead. He helped the children into the wagon, but paused with his hands on her waist.

She squeezed his hands gently. "I know."

He released a low gust of air, then lifted her into the wagon. "Let's get back and pack up. Plenty of busy work to be done before the morning."

"Good thinking." She would be grateful for the distraction. Hopefully between all of them they could distract the children well enough.

Then again, that hardly seemed possible.

Chapter 22

Leanne did one more cursory check to be sure they had everything in line for the arriving stage coach. The coach would be fairly crowded, so Tommy and Nick had offered to ride above. The children had asked to do the same, and Leanne had been loathed to deny them that pleasure, but they'd already decided to take a night in Ogden to refresh themselves before they boarded the train.

After the last stage coach ride, Leanne knew for certain she'd be getting herself a bath. If she were lucky, perhaps Tommy would even join her.

She didn't bother hiding her smile at the idea, especially as Tommy drew close at the moment. Instead of addressing her request, she turned her mind to the last bit of business they needed to cover before they boarded the stage. She glanced at Tommy. "How long until the stage arrives?"

Tommy checked his pocket watch. "Fifteen minutes, give or take. Why?"

"Because we still have one more matter to cover with those girls." She ignored his befuddlement to locate the twins. "Nellie. Flo. Come here, please."

The girls, who had been lounging unceremoniously on the stoop of the store, got to their feet. They trudged over without the excitement of days past. Apparently the stage made everyone grumpy. Flo had the decency to straighten her shoulders and wipe away her frown. "Yes, Miss Leanne? Was there something you needed?"

"We need to have a chat before we get anywhere near Dominion Falls."

Nellie's brow furrowed. "You've gone over the rules with us. We signed a contract. What else could there be to cover?"

"It is about your former teacher, the one that taught you to read. Miss Young? You're aware she was Tommy and Nick's sister, yes?" She waited until they'd both nodded. "You should know what happened to her, and how to react when we get home."

"Wait." Flo turned to Tommy. "She's alive?"

"In a manner of speaking," Tommy admitted.

"But she is not Miss Young any longer." Leanne kept a strong gaze on the two to be sure they listened.

"Of course not, she married that guy. What was his name?" Flo pursed her lips. "Drat."

"Schaffer," Nellie offered.

"It's not Schaffer any longer, either. Clara got herself in a bad way some years ago. A lot happened to her, and in the end, she is no longer Clara." Leanne had expected their confusion, and was even more glad she'd chosen to address the matter before they left. "Her name is Jane Spencer and she remembers nothing beyond five years ago."

Flo outright laughed. "Miss Young didn't forget anything, ever. Trust me, lots of kids wished she did."

"I know she didn't, better than anyone." Tommy's voice grew gruff as it often did when he spoke of Clara. "But she doesn't remember. Any of it. She definitely won't remember you."

"And she doesn't like to be reminded of what she doesn't remember." Leanne stepped closer to the two. "There will be no grand reunion, and you aren't to try to make there be. Jane has more than enough to handle without trying to match up to your memories of her."

Nellie nodded quietly. "We remember. I suppose that is enough." When she met Leanne's gaze, there was a shimmer of unshed tears.

"Really? Nothing? At all?" Flo wasn't quite as willing as her sister to drop the subject. "But she remembered everything."

"She still can, from the time she woke up in Dominion Falls, but no further back." Tommy stepped closer. "She didn't remember her husband, she didn't remember me, her flesh and blood brother. Any of us. There's no tricking her to remember, many have tried. It is what it is. Got it?"

"I suppose." Flo flinched when Nellie elbowed her sharply. "Ow. All right. I understand. We won't say anything."

"Good." Leanne gave a short nod of approval. The stagecoach came over a rise in the distance. "Looks like the stage is here. Let's get our things together and be ready to go."

Tommy took her elbow and guided her away. "Thank you for doing that. Jane would appreciate it if she knew."

"Which she won't. There's no point in telling her."

"Agreed." He nudged his chin toward a nearby bench. "What's going on with Daisy? She's been exceptionally quiet since she got here."

"No idea. The twins made some off-hand comment and she's been upset since. I haven't had time to worry about it, honestly." Leanne sighed. "But it will be a long trip if she remains silent for most of it."

"I think with Flo around, and the children, silence won't be an issue."

"You have a point." As if on cue, the children came running toward them. They both pointed off in the distance toward the stage. Leanne lowered herself to their level. "Yes, that's the stagecoach. It'll take us to the train. I think you'll both really be impressed by the train. We're going to have beds and everything when we get on the train."

Willow's eyes widened. "Beds?"

"Yes. First, we'll have to ride the stage, and that will get hot and stuffy." She squeezed their hands. "Are you both all right?"

Willow nodded weakly, and Jaybird simply shrugged.

"I know it's scary, but I'll be there the whole trip. When we get to Dominion Falls, I won't leave until you're settled. Then I'll see you every day." Leanne got to her feet as the stagecoach pulled up. "Let's go, children. Tommy will get our things."

Jaybird lifted his gaze to watch everything getting loaded onto the roof. When Nick and Tommy took their seats, he frowned. "I want to go up."

"I know. Maybe a little later. Right now, we should all get in the coach." Leanne urged him inside. "We'll see after our first stop, all right?"

Jaybird huffed and crossed his arms. Shivering Willow shrugged and leaned her face out of the window. Leanne took a place between them, happy to see Enid take the spot next to Jaybird.

Their side of the coach was now a little cramped, but it would have to do. Leanne envied the men up top, and couldn't blame Jaybird one bit for wanting to join them.

She sighed and leaned her head back. There was a long ride ahead of them.

* * * *

Tommy had never been so happy to see Dominion Falls. From the window of the train he could just make out a few buildings in the distance until the train curved around a bend. He leaned over and nudged Leanne. "Leanne. We're here."

Leanne groaned awake. "I'm up, I'm up. The children?"

One glance in the bunk above Leanne confirmed his suspicion. "They're up. Staring out the window still. I think they're not about to admit they might be excited by all of this."

"Because they're sad just as much." She glanced toward the bunk above his head. Her smile took on a sad note, but she rose to her feet. "Come on down, you two. We can see things better from another car."

The children climbed down from their bunks without being asked twice. They stuck to Leanne's side though they had the run of the small cabin. Tommy nodded at them both. "Why don't you go on ahead with Leanne? I'll get the others together and ready to go."

Leanne reached out to squeeze his hand. "Thank you. I owe you one."

Tommy grinned at the naughty twist her smile took on. "I'll see to it you make it up to me."

"I have no doubt you will." She laughed as she ushered the children out of the cabin.

Tommy followed them out, but not down the hall. He knocked on every door of their cabins. The whores were already up and chatting heartily. Daisy wasn't in her room, but Nick was in his. He already had his things gathered, and didn't appear surprised at the knock. "Leanne and the children all ready?"

"Yeah. I'm getting the last of our things together. Have you seen Daisy?"

"No." Nick adjusted his glasses. The slightest hint of a pucker at his brow indicated his confusion. "Why would I have? We had separate cabins."

"I know that, she isn't in hers is all. I wasn't sure if you'd seen her." Tommy frowned. "She's been acting odd since Heber City."

"You noticed too, then?" Nick stepped into the corridor. "I didn't want to say anything. I hardly know her. She's all Mike's and Charlie's."

"You've got a point." The train whistle interrupted any further conversation. Tommy stopped in their cabin to grab the satchels before he made his way to where Leanne and the kids were leaning out the window.

By the time the train slowed almost to a stop before the platform, Tommy spotted Jane and Cole waiting. Tommy let Leanne lead the way off the train. He gestured for the whores to follow him out of the train car.

Behind him Flo gasped aloud. "It is her."

"Hush," Nellie chided. She stepped closer to Tommy. "I'm guessing this will take a while. Is there somewhere we can go to wait?"

Tommy nodded, but Nick beat him to the punch. He urged all three whores forward. "We'll take you to the Hangman's Inn. You can get a bite. Leanne, Tommy and the others will be heading there anyhow."

"Thank you, Nick." Tommy moved closer to where Jane appeared to be speaking earnestly with Leanne. "Jane. Cole."

Cole leaned closer while Jane ignored him. "Brought us more strays."

"You always say Jane can't resist," Tommy mumbled. Apparently it wasn't quiet enough as Jane cut him a look. He grinned. "Any leads, Jane?"

"You know perfectly well what leads we have." Jane all but shooed him as she ushered the children to a nearby bench. She sat in front of them and spoke too quiet to be heard, but despite her biting protest to Tommy, she wore a smile.

"So Jane is taking them then?" Tommy glanced at Cole. "You all right with that?"

"It isn't what I expected, but we like that." Cole chuckled. "Just means the next few weeks are going to be awful celibate."

Leanne snorted. "Well good. It should be your turn."

Cole froze when Leanne flounced off, then turned slow to face Tommy. "What the devil does she mean by that?"

Tommy probably should have been intimidated, but he was too amused by the whole situation to bother. "She means we need some alone time without kids. I'm sure you know what that's like." He clapped Cole on the shoulder and strode over to the bench before Cole could react.

Cole wasn't far behind. Instead of approaching Tommy again, he leaned down and whispered in Jane's ear.

Jane paused briefly to focus on Tommy. "About time. Now, how about we get you two fed? Willow, Jaybird? You'll be able to meet more people at the hotel, but we'll take it slow."

Willow took Jane's offered hand hesitantly. Jaybird stared at the other for several long seconds.

Jane leaned down to Jaybird with a smile. "We have some of the best venison you've had—and if you eat up, I might be convinced to part with one of my sweetcakes. Leanne said you rather enjoyed those."

Jaybird took her hand without another heartbeat of a pause.

Tommy held Leanne back for a few seconds. "Travelling really does not bode well for your temperament, does it?"

"Neither does losing my Virgin Madam status only to not be able to indulge in such pleasures again since."

"So shall we then?"

"Once the children are settled."

"You're killing me."

"No, I'm killing us both."

Epilogue

Leanne sat quiet as a mouse at a table in Jane's apartment. After three days of near constant visitation to ensure the children were settled into their new home. For the moment Jaybird played checkers with Sally, while Willow tried her hand at drawing with some of the tools Alma had shared.

Jane sank into the seat opposite Leanne. "They're settling in fine. I suppose the question now is if you're ready to let go."

"It's so difficult for Willow to trust. I'm only worried about letting her down." Leanne smiled over at her friend. "I do have a life I am eager to return to. Three new whores to be sure are keeping in line."

"Then go. There will be adjustments here, but you'll still see her plenty. It isn't like you aren't here all the time. I see you nearly as much as Kat, who lives across the street." Jane grinned, "And I imagine now that you and Thomas have finally crossed that line I'll be seeing you more when he's around."

"Perhaps." Leanne didn't have much luck hiding her pleasure at the idea.

"I'm very happy for you both, you know."

"Thank you. Just please, don't expect much. This is all new to me."

"Hey." Jane set her hand on Leanne's. "I promise, there will be none of that. I simply wanted the two of you to stop getting in your own way. From here on out, I have too much going on for me to pester you for anything else. If you and Thomas are happy, that's what matters to me most."

"Thank heavens."

"Now go. Find my brother, take care of your whores. I will handle the children. Slip out before they notice. Go. Shoo."

Leanne didn't wait for Jane to physically shoo her out the door. She slipped out before either of the children saw her move. All the way through the hotel she kept an eye peeled for Tommy, but to no avail.

Outside she finally spotted him a few doors away. She rushed toward him, meeting his grin with one of her own. "Good afternoon."

"Afternoon." He eyed her up and down before meeting her gaze. "You're not attached to any children."

"I'm not."

"So what are you planning to do?"

"Well, I have some whores to deal with." She chuckled when his shoulders sank. "However, I was hoping that I might spend some time with you first."

"I'd be honored." He offered her his arm. "Where to?"

"Anywhere. I'm all yours."

To Be

Continued...

In the rest of

The

Dominion

Falls Series

About the

Author

Sarah Cass, author of over twenty novels in 4 series, is devoted to giving her readers well-crafted, emotional stories, with depth to even her secondary characters—to give readers a full world to explore. Stories that explore not only the labyrinths of the heart, but the nightmares of the soul. A RONE finalist, she is also owner and creator of Redefining Perfect. By day, she's a nurse, a mother, wife and cat-mom to 4 mischievous beasts. By night she crafts stories that take her across centuries. From the old west of Dominion Falls, to the small town of Lake Point for the holidays, and even into the paranormal land of Shifters and Magic in The Tribe. She loves hearing from her readers. Visit her at www.authorsarahcass.com

Other Books in
The Dominion Falls Series

Independent Brake
Changing Tracks
Derailed
Dark Territory
Green Eye
Runaway Train
Home Signal

Coming Soon in
The Dominion Falls Series

Dust Raiser
Chase the Red
Blizzard Lights
Dead Man's Switch
Bird Cage
A Highball Arrangement
Douse the Glim
Blood
Grave Digger
Bad Order

Books by Sarah Cass

The Tribe Series
The Tribe
The Wolf
The Chief
The Raven
The Lake Point Series
Santa, Maybe
Deep-Fried Sweethearts
Stalled Independence
Witch Way
A Thorough Thanksgiving
Eve's New Year
Heartstrings & Hockey Pucks
Luck of the Cowgirl
Stars, Stripes & Motorbikes
Free Falling
Love for Hire
Haunted Hearts
Stand Alone Novels
Masked Hearts
Leap